DO NOT OPEN

KIERSTEN MODGLIN

KIERSTEN
MODGLIN

Cover Design by Kiersten Modglin
Copy Editing by Three Owls Editing
Proofreading by My Brother's Editor
Formatting by Kiersten Modglin
Copyright © 2023 by Kiersten Modglin.
All rights reserved.

First Print and Electronic Edition: 2023
kierstenmodglinauthor.com

For every single one of us doing hard and brave things every single day. Chasing dreams, healing, trying, believing, fighting, hoping.
I see you, I'm rooting for you,
and I hope you're so proud of yourself.

"One feather is of no use to me, I must have the whole bird."

JAKOB GRIMM, *THE GOLDEN BIRD*

CHAPTER ONE

I'm brushing vomit from my teeth when the email arrives. A single phone chime that does nothing to let me know how much it will change my life.

I assume it's a reader asking when they can expect my latest book. Those are coming more and more frequently now. I suppose I should be flattered—or at the very least grateful—for this, but mostly it just reminds me that I'm failing.

That I'm letting more people down.

My current manuscript sits on my laptop at around thirteen thousand words. Twelve thousand—give or take —of which are pure garbage. I haven't touched it in weeks, and when I do, it's just to stare at the page and contemplate changing my characters' names. *Again.*

I've lost my touch. Lost my motivation. Lost my ability to care about anything at all, but especially characters that don't truly exist dealing with problems that also don't exist.

I just can't bring myself to do it anymore.

Ever since...

No.

I force the thought away, grabbing the bottle of vodka sitting next to my sink. I'm not going to have too much to drink. It's only eleven in the morning, after all, but I feel so bad already, I think a sip or two won't hurt.

Lifting the bottle to my lips, I welcome the familiar burn and pick up my phone to check the email.

From: Owen Doyle
To: Mari@MariettaMorgan.com
Subject: Hello!

I roll my eyes. *Hello, Owen Doyle. What the hell do you want?*

Opening the email, I realize it's not a reader, but a scammer. *Even better.*

Hi Mari!

I hope this email finds you well. I wanted to reach out to say what huge fans my wife and I are of your work. We read them together quite often and we're always floored at how easily you're able to blow us away with your twists! We've yet to predict any of them. In fact, we just finished *No Chance* last night and we were

both sure we had it figured out for the first time, only to be blown away when you brought Brady back at the last minute! Brilliant!

Anyway, we've just moved to Charleston, and I wondered if you'd ever be up for meeting us for coffee or something? It would make her day, and I'd get major cool points. I'm also an award-winning producer of films and television shows like *Last Revenge*, *Death Day*, and *Say You Will*. I'm linking my website below. I'd love to discuss working together in the future!

Hope to hear back from you.

Best,
Owen

I sigh. If I had a dollar for every time I got an email from some "production company" interested in turning one of my books into a film (for the low, low cost of ten thousand dollars), I'd never need to write another book again.

I almost close the email. *Almost.*

But curiosity gets the best of me. Even with alcohol still coursing through my system from last night, I'm not stupid enough to click any links in the email. Instead, I open my browser and search the name of his production company.

Epic Scope Productions

I expect to find a shoddy website with one or two pages of random film posters, but what I find instead actually looks to be legit. In fact, they've produced some of my favorite shows and movies. I click on the "About" section and see the company was founded by Owen Doyle more than ten years ago.

Setting the bottle of vodka back on the counter, I read through the numerous articles discussing the work they're doing and how they're bringing new stories and new voices to the screen.

I glance up at the oversized bathroom mirror in front of me, staring at my ruddy skin and the dark bags under my eyes. Could I be dreaming somehow?

Could this guy be for real?

I open social media next, but he doesn't seem to have accounts on any of the platforms. Not unusual from what I know of Hollywood. There are a few Owen Doyle accounts that I skim through, but only two real contenders. One has a photo of the sky as his profile photo, but his account is mostly landscape shots. The other has a photo of a man and woman standing next to each other in front of a theater, but his account is private.

If he's either one of these Owens, I'll learn nothing from the profiles.

I go back to the email, reading over it once more. He mentioned my latest book and knew parts of the plot, which has me hesitantly considering the fact that this might be a real email.

I check the email server which also seems real. **@epicscopeprod.com**

It seems too good to be true, though. Right?

I mean, this isn't how it works. Especially not for writers like me.

While I have a respectable following, I've never made it onto any of the bestseller lists, none of my books have been celebrity book club picks, and I can name hundreds of authors more successful than I am that he could reach out to instead.

Still, my finger hovers over the reply button.

What's the worst that could happen?

If I respond and he asks for money, I'll know the truth either way. Deciding to stop second-guessing, I exit the bathroom and seek out my laptop on the nightstand next to the bed. On the off chance this is real, I want to be sure my email is well-crafted.

I read through the email two more times before writing my response, trying to find the perfect blend of cool and casual.

Hey Owen,
So nice to hear from you. I love to hear you and your wife—

Or is it your wife and you? You guys? You all? Ugh. Delete.

Hey Owen,
So nice to hear from you. I love to hear you've
enjoyed my stories.

Is "novels" better? "Books"? "Thrillers"? Delete.

Hey Owen,

It's great to hear from you, and thank you for
checking out my work. I'm thrilled you've
enjoyed it. Super cool that you're local. I'd
definitely be up for meeting for coffee. Just let
me know what your schedule looks like.

Best,
Mari

Oh. Shoot. Will he think I'm copying his sign off?
Delete.

Warmest wishes,
Mari

No, too formal.

Talk soon,
Mari

There. That will have to do. It takes so much effort to

appear effortless. Before I press send, I read over it twice, then again out loud. I toy with the idea of telling him I'm a fan of his work, too, but decide against it. I don't want to seem like I'm sucking up.

Whatever. Who cares? It's probably a scam anyway.

Send.

CHAPTER TWO

"I mean, it's been a week. Like I said, it was probably a scam. Either that, or he emailed the wrong author. Or there was a typo in my email, and he realized I'm a terrible fraud who mixes up 'their,' 'there,' and 'they're,' and he doesn't want to work with someone so incompetent."

The last one is impossible, I know. I've read that email twenty additional times since I sent it. There were no typos.

I pour wine into two glasses and hand one to Kassara.

"*Or*," she offers in a sing-song voice, "he's just been busy and hasn't had a chance to get back with you."

I give a look that says, *get on board with my pessimism or get out*. Luckily for me, Kassara is well-versed in, and completely immune, to my cynicism and terrible personality.

I'm not sure why she's still here, honestly. She's much too sunshiney to enjoy being around someone like me.

But then again, what do I know? *Show me back to my dark corner, sir.*

I'll stop mentally rambling now. That's the burden of being a writer, truly. We spend so much time in our heads, we rarely experience the world outside of it. Not in the same way other people do.

"Maybe," I say finally. "Anyway, how was your trip?"

"Fine." She takes a sip of her wine as we make our way back to the living room. "When you've been to one conference, you've been to them all." Her eyes narrow, and I sense an impending question. "Speaking of, when are you planning to start coming with me again? You keep putting it off."

I flop down on the couch, careful not to spill a single drop of wine. It's not even the good stuff, but still too precious to waste. "Um, I don't know. Probably, like, never."

"Why?" She studies me, sitting down carefully. Kassara works for one of the largest audiobook companies in the country. It's how we met—at a writing conference I attended what feels like a lifetime ago. When we realized she'd just moved to Charleston from Chicago, our friendship felt like fate. She's probably—definitely—been the only thing keeping me going over this past year. "You said you would try this year. I think it could be really good for you to get out and see people again. Everyone is always asking about you."

"Like you said, if you've been to one, you've been to them all."

She doesn't look happy, but she doesn't push the issue any further. "Okay. Well, have you been working?"

"Yes," I lie. "A lot, actually. Busy, busy."

"Can I see what you have so far?"

She knows the answer to that, so I don't entertain the question. "What are you reading lately? Anything good?"

"Murder as always," she says, lifting the remote and browsing one of the many streaming services I'm subscribed to. "I've been listening to the new Lisa Regan book. What about you? Read anything good?"

Do the backs of wine bottles count? I don't say that. Kassara knows about my drinking, but she doesn't know the extent of it. Like any good alcohol enthusiast, I keep it hidden well, even from my best friend. "Not really. I've picked up a few things, but nothing's really held my attention. So, I go back to *Gilmore Girls* for the umpteenth time instead." My phone chimes from beside me on the end table, and my heart skips a beat. It's been doing that all week, but like all the other times, I'm positive this won't be a reply from Owen. It'll be a sale from a shoe store I used to love or a receipt from my recurring wine delivery subscription.

When I look at the screen, I have to do a double take. "Oh my god. It's him."

Kassara turns her head to face me, cautious optimism in her eyes. "Him who?"

"It's Owen Doyle. The producer."

She squeals, placing her glass down, and launches forward. "What'd he say? What'd he say?"

My phone takes forever to load the email, but when it

finally does, I read his response aloud. "Mari, this is so exciting. We are looking forward to it. How does the thirtieth look for your schedule? We'll both be in town that day, and we'd love to have you to our place for dinner and drinks instead if that works for you? If not, just let us know what would. We're looking forward to it! Owen."

I glance up at Kassara, whose grin is practically blinding. She grabs my arm and squeezes. "Oh my god, Mari! This is real! Oh my god! You're going to go meet with a Hollywood producer! Holy cow!"

Her excitement is infectious, but I fight against it, a growing sense of worry looming in the pit of my stomach.

"What's wrong?" she asks, sensing my hesitation.

"I don't know. What if I make myself look dumb? What if I'm not fancy enough? I don't know anything about Hollywood. Besides that, I haven't spoken to anyone aside from you in a year. I'm socially awkward. I'm going to ruin this somehow. I should just say I can't make it and slowly blow him off, right?"

She shakes her head, taking my phone from my hand and placing both of her palms on my arms. "Oh, absolutely not. He's the one who reached out to you. He said he's a huge fan. What have you got to be nervous about? You don't have to impress him by doing anything other than what you've already done. Writing killer books. He knows you aren't in Hollywood. He isn't expecting you to be an expert on his job. He just wants you to be you. Maybe he'll be the one embarrassing himself when he fangirls over his favorite author."

I roll my eyes, looking away doubtfully. "Yeah, okay.

I'm sure he was just being polite. Besides, I hate to break it to you, but the *me* who wrote those books he loves so much is long gone and buried."

Sympathy fills her eyes, and she opens her mouth as if she already had an argument ready but closes it again. "Look, I know. I know it's scary, but you'll be fine. He's asking to meet you, not the other way around. A legitimate film producer is interested in meeting with you. *You*, Mari. That's a huge deal. If you don't go, someone else will. How many other authors would kill to be in your position? What if, let's just say, you don't respond?" She purses her lips, twirling her wrist in thought. "It's fine. It's okay. You'll move on. Forget about it. Wonder *what if,* sure, but you can deal with that. But what if maybe, just maybe, he reaches out to Darlene Cosgrove to talk about her books next? How would you feel if you learned they went out to dinner and had a great time? If they became friends? If he turned one of her nonsense books into a movie? Can you honestly tell me you'd be okay with that?"

Bitterness creeps into my chest. She knows how I feel about Darlene Cosgrove—how fake she is, how she pretends to be something we both know she's not. If I pass up this opportunity and it's handed to my arch enemy, I'd never forgive myself. Besides that, I can't deny the allure of having any of my books turned into a film or television show. The idea that my books could be brought to life in such a way is mesmerizing. Not so long ago, I used to lie awake and dream up casts, imagining who would play which character. This sort of thing is rare. Hollywood producers don't just reach out to midlist authors and ask them for coffee. It's so unheard of, in fact, I'd hate myself for letting it pass me by.

Decision made, I nod. "Fine. You're right. It's a huge opportunity. And, if we don't click, at least I tried. There's no harm in meeting him."

"You don't have to be anyone but yourself. Pretend he's just another reader. You're never nervous to meet them."

"Readers are different. They get me. They *like* me." At least, they like the person I used to be.

"He's a reader, too, though, Mari. Just remember that, and you'll be fine."

I glance down at the email again. "Should I agree to go to his house? That feels a little strange, doesn't it? Maybe I'll ask if we can stick with the original plan and meet for coffee instead..."

"I don't know. What if that comes across as rude?" she asks, touching a finger to her bottom lip thoughtfully.

"Would it? He offered that first. I could just say I'd feel more comfortable meeting for coffee. Or just brush off the invitation to his house and say, 'Let's meet at Mudhouse,' or something."

She nods slowly, eyes searching the air. "Yeah, I guess that would be okay. Maybe don't say you'd feel more comfortable not going to his house. That might come off wrong and make him feel weird. Just word it differently somehow..."

"Well, now you have me second-guessing," I point out, lowering my phone. This time, I'll send my response from here, not my computer. That's how cool and casual I am. *See? Totally effortless.*

"I'm sure it would be fine to go to his house. I mean, famous people want their privacy, right? Besides, what if you need to talk business? You don't want to do that in public."

"I hardly think he's going to make some crazy offer when we meet for the first time," I say, though I have no idea how Hollywood-types work. Maybe this *is* normal after all. "He may just want to say hello and tell me he's enjoyed my books. For all I know, he's going to do some documentary on what happened to Declan and Liam and is just luring me there to get my take on it."

"Oh, stop. He is not." She gives me a look. After a beat, she says, "It's up to you, I guess. Whatever you're most comfortable with." She's convincing, but I can tell what she thinks is right. I know she thinks I'm on the verge of scaring him off.

Maybe I am. Maybe it wouldn't be the worst thing if I did.

Even as I think it, though, I know I'm lying to myself. I want this to work out more than I'm willing to admit.

"If it were you, you'd just say yes to his offer?"

She sucks in a breath, speaking slowly. "If it were me, I'd take him up on the offer to meet at his house, yes. I don't really see the harm. If he were to try anything, it's not like we don't know who he is. He's a huge name. He's not going to risk his reputation. Besides, his wife will be there, and you'll be able to give me the address. I'm not sure what the other risks would be. It'll be like we're young and hip and going on first dates. You can text me when you get there to let me know it's safe, but if I don't hear from you, I'll call the police. You could even wear one of those bracelets Declan got you before. The one where you tap to let the other person know you're thinking of them. Except this time it would be to let me know you're alive. One tap, I'm safe and sound and on my way to stardom. Two taps, I'm locked in a concrete room. Save me."

It's a joke, but I don't like it. Besides, if Declan's bracelet still exists, it's likely packed away or lost, and I don't have time to order a new set before the date Owen has proposed.

"Funny." I let out a breath. As she's saying it, it sounds ridiculous. This is a high-powered film executive. He's not going to do anything to harm me. More important than his address, Kassara has his name. If he knew the mental gymnastics I'm going through over whether or not he's dangerous, he'd likely withdraw his offer and never speak to me again.

Be cooler than this, Mari.

I type out a response quickly, letting him know that I'd be happy to come for a visit at his home and I'll be free that day. I pass the phone to Kassara for her to read over it and, when she's done, she presses send before I can overthink it and tosses the phone back to me. She elbows me gently as I lock the screen, taking a large gulp of my wine and wishing it was something stronger.

"They'd be really proud of you, you know?" she says gently, and I don't have to ask whom she's talking about.

"Well, they aren't here, are they?" My voice sounds more bitter than I mean for it to—as bitter as this cheap wine.

She looks down, unbothered by my tone.

They never will be again.

Before I can set down my empty wineglass, my phone screen lights up with an incoming email. I'd expected to wait days for a response like last time. Could it be him again already?

Kassara leans toward me to look, too, and I open up the email and read the address he's sent, along with the proposed time for our meeting.

3 p.m. work for you?

A perfectly safe time. Not yet dark. Not late enough for anything nefarious to happen. It instantly puts me at ease.

When I read the address again, something flutters in my chest. *Holy cow.*

They live on Sullivan's Island.

No doubt in a mansion that would fit my entire house in one of its closets. "Am I really doing this?" I ask gently. Lately, I'm never sure when things are actually happening and when I'm in one of my liquor-soaked dreams. Seeing Declan and Liam again are the only give-aways when I've left reality for the moment.

"No going back now," Kassara says with a gleam in her eyes. "October thirtieth is next week. We have to go shopping!"

Somehow, I wish I was dreaming.

CHAPTER THREE

When I pull up to the oceanfront mansion, I'm both relieved it seems to be safe and utterly intimidated all at once. Nothing about this is normal. Two weeks ago, I was a simple person living an average—albeit miserable and lonely—life. Now, I'm meeting with a Hollywood producer who's a *big fan* of my work, apparently.

Things like this don't happen to people like me.

I'm trying to be positive about all of this. Truly, I am. I realize this is an opportunity so many authors, most more talented than I am, would kill for. I realize I'm living a dream that, two years ago, I would've celebrated. A dream Declan and I fantasized about, a dream we worked so hard for. The problem is, back then, I would've had my husband and son to celebrate with me. Declan likely would've accompanied me to the meeting.

Now, I'm alone.

I feel the weight of that even more as I step out of the

car and walk toward the door. I want to turn around and dart back, run for home and make up some excuse as to why I couldn't make it.

Food poisoning.

Car trouble.

Bird flu.

Something. Anything.

But I can't. I won't.

Darlene Cosgrove would eat this opportunity up, and so will I. I will make my family proud in whatever way they still can be. I will get the dream I still have left. Who knows? Maybe I'll find happiness again by getting it. That feels impossible, but I've learned to never use that word.

I square my shoulders toward the front door, aware I'm likely being watched right now from somewhere inside the house. Then again, maybe not. Not everyone is as bored and paranoid as I am.

For all I know, Owen's on his weekly video call with Jason Bateman and the entire cast of *Friends*, and I'll be greeted by his housekeeper.

My heels click across the concrete as I make my way up the long walk and stop to take in the sight of the house. I admit, I did a little digging. Turns out Owen Doyle relocated from LA to the Charleston area last year, selling his fourteen-million-dollar home and no doubt upgrading with this one, which is now on the market again for twenty-five million. At twelve thousand square feet, perhaps it's too small for the lavish parties he's well known for throwing.

The house is breathtaking, though it looks out of place here next to the more traditional beach houses. This one appears as if it's been brought over from Italy, with sweeping, stone staircases running down either side of the large balcony in the front. It's the color of sand, with massive windows and peaks everywhere you look.

Before I forget, I quickly pull out my phone, sending Kassara a text to let her know I've arrived.

> Just got here. House is unreal. Wish me luck!

I turn around at the creaking sound behind me, noticing the double iron gates closing on either side of the circular driveway. They'd been open when I arrived, so I had hardly noticed them.

Now I know for sure he knows I'm here, so I should stop gawking and get to the front door.

Kassara's response arrives as I make my way up the walk.

> You've got this! Don't forget about us little people!

I snort and tuck the phone back into my purse, nearing the door. Upon reaching it, I knock on the wood, then immediately begin to question if it was loud enough.

Should I knock again? But if it was loud enough and he heard me, a second knock would seem impatient. Then again, if he didn't hear me, he must be wondering what the heck is taking so long.

I notice the bronze doorbell to my right and internally kick myself. Obviously, I should've rung the bell, but I can't do that now.

Maybe I should send him an email to let him know I've arrived? Maybe I should—

The door swings open, and my questions stop.

"Mari." The man in front of me exudes warmth, wealth, and confidence. He's average height with alabaster skin, spiky black hair, and small, round glasses. If Ben Linus from *Lost* had a twin, this would be him. I'm relieved to finally put a face with a name since I hadn't been able to find any photos of him online. "It's so nice to finally meet you." He holds out both arms, dismissing my awkwardly outstretched hand to pull me in for a hug. "Come in, come in."

It lasts only seconds, and then he steps back, allowing me to come inside. The house is like a museum, soaked in sunlight from the enormous windows. The walls, floors, ceilings, and staircases are all made of stone and marble. The furniture is a mix of classic and modern, and I get the feeling the table in the hall costs more than my mortgage.

"Thank you. It's nice to meet you, too," I say, snapping my eyes back to his when I realize I still haven't spoken. "Thank you again for having me. You have a beautiful home."

He shoves his hands into his pockets. "Charleston's a lovely area, isn't it? My wife and I came here to visit a friend a few summers ago and fell in love with it."

"So, are you here full-time now?" *Is that rude to ask? Why should he want me to know where he lives?*

Because he's the one who invited you, I hear Kassara's voice silencing my panic.

"We're back and forth between here and LA. And my production company has an office in Atlanta. So, all over the place, but this is home now, yes." He leads me through the foyer and into a small sitting room, where I see a tray of drinks waiting. My throat goes dry at the sight. "What about you? Your website said you live in Charleston, but it didn't say if this is where you're from originally."

"Yeah, I'm not. My husband and I moved here right after our son was born. I grew up in Savannah, though, so not *too* far away."

"Your husband?" He checks behind me. "Is he with you?"

"Oh. Um, no." My voice catches, and I clear my throat, passing it off as a cough. I'm surprised he doesn't know what happened. "He's not... I mean, he's... It's just me now."

"I see." He doesn't offer his condolences, which I'm somehow grateful for. Perhaps because he doesn't know whether he should. I didn't exactly elaborate on what happened to him, but he seems to understand. Instead, he leans down and picks up both glasses from the tray and passes one to me. "I hope you don't mind. I made us my signature cocktail, a boulevardier." The amber liquid sloshes in the glass as I stare down into it.

"Not at all. It looks delicious." Like a proper addict, my entire body is now buzzing with adrenaline, the drink in my hand the only thing I can focus on. I haven't allowed myself a drink all day, and every nerve in my body is screaming in revolt. Demanding a sip, like a petulant toddler. I lift the cocktail to my lips and take a small drink. In an instant, everything in me goes electric. My brain seems to whir to life. The room around me is brighter. "And it is," I say with a laugh, and even to my own ears, it sounds charming. I glance down at the tray again. "Only two glasses? What about your wife?"

Why did I ask that? I let a moment of confidence get the best of me. *Maybe she doesn't drink. Maybe she's pregnant.* Either way, it's none of my business.

"Ah." He sighs, looking away regretfully. "I'm sorry to say Audrey couldn't make it today after all. She got a call early this morning about one of our productions and had to head to the office in LA to deal with that. It's killing her not to be here."

"Oh. I'm sad she couldn't be, but I totally understand. I wouldn't have minded rescheduling, though." I wish I could rescind the words the second they leave my mouth. *Was that rude? Do I sound like I don't want to be here? Like I would've rather rescheduled?*

He simply smiles and adjusts his glasses. "Well, hopefully this will be the first of many meetings, and you'll see each other soon." He turns his head, nodding in the direction of the doorway. "Come on, I want to show you why we picked this place."

I follow him out of the sitting room—there's probably a fancier name for it, but I have no idea what it is—and down a hall. We pass through the large chef's kitchen with double islands, and I try not to stare. Past the kitchen is a grand, enclosed piazza overlooking the ocean. I can't help the gasp that escapes my lips, and he looks over at me.

"Beautiful, isn't it?"

"Wow," I murmur. "It really is."

He chuckles. "Almost like the setting of one of your brilliant books."

My cheeks heat.

One corner of his mouth upturns and he shoves a hand into his pocket with a sigh. "They are, you know. Brilliant. I've never found an author whose books make me feel the way yours do. The twists manage to get me every time. How do you do that?" He turns to face me.

"It's fun for me, honestly," I say, giving the answer I have prepared for whenever a podcast host or moderator on a panel asks the question. "It's fun for me to plot through the eyes of a reader and try to figure out what you'll be guessing, so I can lead you off course and down the wrong path."

He grins and takes another sip of his drink. So do I, this time allowing myself to suck down even more of the liquid. My body is buzzing like a pulse. *More. More. More.*

I have to pace myself. Whatever happens, I'll never live it down if I embarrass myself today. I take another sip, trying to appease the internal begging.

"You were born for it, obviously. Is it what you've always wanted to do? Write, I mean?" To my shock, it's he who looks embarrassed. "Sorry, you must get asked that question all the time."

"It's okay." I don't tell him I do, in fact, get asked that often because it's an easy question to answer. I'll take all the easy questions I can get. "It's a good question. I've always known, yeah. I've wanted to be a writer for as long as I can remember." I venture a bit of bravery and ask, "Which of my books is your favorite?"

He stares back at the ocean with a chuckle. "Hm. That's a tough one."

For a brief moment, I wonder if he's actually read any of them. Perhaps his secretary crafted the email. Maybe he's been lying this whole time.

"I'd say it's a tie between *Deadly Games* and *For You I Would*. *Deadly Games* because it's your debut and the first one I read of yours, but *For You I Would* easily had the best twist I've ever read. I mean, the fact that we didn't realize the POV trickery until the end..." He kisses his fingertips like a chef. "I still haven't quite figured out how you pulled that one off. I thought for sure Donovan was the killer."

I smile, my belly bubbling with pride. "Thank you. That's one of my favorites, too. I didn't actually have that twist figured out until near the end of the first draft."

"No kidding?"

I nod, taking another drink.

"I can't wait to tell Audrey that."

"What about you?" I ask. "Have you always wanted to work in film and television?"

His head tilts to the side slowly. "Well, I wanted to be an actor first. But I always knew I wanted to do something with film, yes. So, when acting didn't pan out, producing was something that intrigued me. Luckily, it was a good fit." He glances up at the house around us as if to say it worked out pretty well. "Would you like some more?" He points to my glass, which is empty. I'd hardly noticed I drank it all. "Then we can sit down and chat before dinner's ready. We're having lamb. I hope that's okay."

I've only had lamb once while on a family vacation, so my mind instantly goes to Declan and Liam, but I ignore the pain, forcing images of their smiling faces away. My drink can't be refilled fast enough. "Sounds delicious."

He takes my glass from me, and we head for the kitchen. As he prepares my drink, I send Kassara another quick text.

Made it inside. Still alive and well.

"So, where do you live, Mari?"

"Downtown," I tell him, shoving my phone back into my purse, embarrassed to see he's caught me on it. "Near Westside."

He nods, not revealing if he knows the area, and passes my glass back to me. I glance down at the island, studying the marble veining. Slowly, I trace a finger across it. "You have a beautiful home." *Did I already say that?*

"Thank you." His voice is slower this time, like he's mulling over the words. Suddenly, there's a sharp ache in the back of my head. I no longer feel electric. Instead, I feel as if I'm static. The buzzing in me has begun to dull. I take another drink, trying to bring myself back.

This is not the time to lose it. I need to be here. Be present.

I've never felt this way, like my nerves are pulling me down. Like I'm sinking. I place the glass on the island, terrified I'll drop it. I picture the glass shattering around my feet in slow motion.

"Mari? Is everything alright?" He says the words, but there's no emotion in his voice.

I can barely hear him.

What's happening?

I put a hand to my chest, searching for my heartbeat as the room begins to spin. I feel drunk—though I haven't had nearly enough to drink—and like I'm having a panic attack all at once. "I don't... I'm so sorry. I don't feel so well."

"Maybe you should sit down." He takes hold of my arm, but it's too late. I feel myself slipping. And then, before I know what's happening, everything—him, me, the house—it all disappears. There is only black.

CHAPTER FOUR

When I open my eyes, the world is fuzzy and unfamiliar. I'm not sure where I am or why I'm here. My head is heavy and throbbing, like I've had too much to drink, and my throat feels like sandpaper.

I stare around, blinking and rubbing my eyes as I sit up in a bed I don't remember getting into. My mind scours my memories, searching for anything familiar. The room is dark and humid, with an earthy smell, and there are no windows in any of the concrete walls. The space is illuminated by only a single lamp next to the bed, giving the air an amber glow. It feels like the basement in my cousin's house in Illinois, but it's so rare to find a basement here in Charleston, I know that can't be it.

Unless I'm no longer in Charleston.

How did I end up here?

The last thing I remember is...meeting Owen. What happened after I left? *Did* I leave? Did I do something to embarrass myself in front of him?

Mortification swells in my chest as I search for memories that don't exist. I lift the covers off my legs and slip out of bed.

Perhaps I'm still dreaming. Maybe Kassara's jokes about being locked in a concrete room have gotten to my head. The floor beneath my feet does seem to be concrete, after all, though it has been covered with thin, cheap carpet. It's uncomfortable and cold as I walk across it. I search for my purse or my phone, but neither appear to be in this room. My bladder burns for relief, and I head for the door.

My worst fear at this moment is that the meeting with Owen didn't go well, and I got drunk afterward to soothe my hurt ego. Perhaps I went home with someone at a bar, which would explain this strange location. But I prefer to drink at home alone, so that would be out of character.

I approach the metal door cautiously, studying the rough texture of the jade-green paint on its surface. On the wall next to the door, there's a single lightswitch. I lift a hand to flip it on. Over the bed, the small light fixture mounted to the ceiling comes on, though one of the two bulbs inside of it is burned out so the fixture illuminates the space only somewhat better than the lamp.

I turn back to the door and grab the knob, twisting it quickly, my throat tense at the possibility of what I might find on the outside, but...nothing happens.

I twist again.

Nothing.

No.

Nothing.

Nothing.

Nothing.

The door is stuck. *Locked.*

I am locked inside.

Panic washes over me like a tidal wave. A sharp, gravitational pull of terror. *Why am I locked inside this room?* I tug on the handle harder, pressing my foot to the doorframe for leverage.

"Hello?" I shout, banging my fist onto the door rapidly. I spin around, looking for another way out, for a way to pry this door open, but there is nothing.

Just as I feel as if my lungs may collapse, the door swings open, a gust of wind sweeping over me, and Owen appears.

He's changed his clothes—now dressed in jeans and a plain black shirt—and he grins at me as if everything is fine. Because I still don't understand what's going on, I feel an apology clawing at the back of my throat. How silly must I look?

"Owen," I say his name on a breath. "I'm so sorry. I'm... The door was stuck." I glance around. "Is everything okay? What's going on? Where am I?"

He steps forward, blocking the doorway. "Mari, thank goodness you're awake. I was so worried. You don't remember anything that happened?"

Heat hits my cheeks. What must he think of me? That I'm some drunk who can't make it through a meeting without making a fool of myself? "I... Some parts are fuzzy. I must've had a bad reaction to one of the drinks..." The last word of my sentence comes out slowly as I begin to realize what's happening. What *may* be happening, because I have no proof just yet. Owen wouldn't have drugged me, would he? Internally, I do an assessment of my body. I don't feel sore or hurt in any way, just tired and sort of out of it.

"You passed out in the kitchen," he says gently, embarrassed for me. "I tried to wake you up, but you were still so groggy. I brought you down here to rest."

"I don't understand..." I put a hand to my head. "I've never done anything like that before." It's a lie, but my passing out is always directly related to my drinking, and a single drink—even a strong one—is nothing to me. Something else must've happened. Maybe my nerves got the best of me, but even that feels unlikely. I just don't want my suspicion to be true.

"It was very strange. You had me worried. Luckily, I got to you before you hit the floor. Are you...feeling alright now?" His eyes are sort of bugged out, like he's expecting me to keel over again at any moment.

"Yes," I say, still feeling uneasy. "Much better, thank you. I'm so sorry about all of this. I can't tell you how embarrassed I am." I move toward the door, but he sidesteps, stopping me.

"No need to be embarrassed."

"Right." My eyes flick to the small space between him and the open doorway. If I try to get to it, I'll run into him. "Well, I should really be going. Maybe we can plan to do this again when your wife is back home. I'll be sure to eat something beforehand." I giggle nervously. "I'm sure it was just a combination of nerves and low blood sugar."

"There's no rush to run off." He pushes the door closed, his eyes flicking over me. "Why don't you sit down for a second, and let's make sure you're okay. You shouldn't be driving if you're feeling unwell." His hands come to my upper arms, and he nudges me backward.

It's such a strange thing. On the one hand, I'm freaking out and terrified about what's happening, but on the other, nothing is actually happening, and I don't want to cause a scene or more embarrassment to myself by not complying. So, I find myself edging backward until the backs of my knees hit the bed. I ease myself down until I'm sitting, almost in a trance. "I'm fine, really. What time is it? It must be getting late."

He doesn't answer. Instead, he walks around me and runs a hand over a bowl on the nightstand that I hadn't noticed. "Did you notice I got your favorites?" I look over just in time to see him pick up a single purple hard candy. "Grape LifeSavers. I know how much you love them." There must be one hundred of them in the bowl. More than I could eat in several days. Several weeks, maybe.

"That's really kind of you." I swallow, standing again, but he darts forward, blocking my exit.

"You should sit, Mari. It's really not safe for you to be standing right now. You don't look so good."

I remain standing. "No. I'm okay. Really. I appreciate your concern, but I should be getting back now. My friend will be worried about me. I'm supposed to be meeting her to sign some papers that are time-sensitive. If I don't show up, she'll start to worry. She's a bit overprotective. I'd hate for her to call the police and report me missing or something." I try to laugh.

"*But—*" His voice is too loud, so he stops, pinching the bridge of his nose and closing his eyes. He starts again, "You can't leave yet. Look at all the effort I went through to make sure you're comfortable. All of your favorites." He gestures around the room, pointing to the stack of old horror DVDs and a bowl of peaches. "I have a bottle of chardonnay upstairs chilling, too."

"Oh. Wow." I assume I'm failing to hide my shock. I have no idea how he knows my favorite things. Though I'm sure I've mentioned my love of grape-flavored candies and white wine in interviews, as well as mentioned several old horror movies in my books, this feels...stalkerish. "That's so nice."

"Oh, I didn't even show you the best part." His eyes light up as he pulls open the drawer to the nightstand, and every muscle in my body tenses. "Fuzzy socks." He pulls out a handful of them. "You said once in an interview you can't write without fuzzy socks. I made sure to get several, so you'd feel more comfortable."

I force a smile. "You really know your stuff."

"I know everything about you," he says, his voice somehow both whimsical and stern.

"You didn't need to go through all this trouble. It's very kind. Really, though, I should be going." I head for the door, but he grabs me, his grip too tight.

"Owen, please..." I whimper. *This is happening. This is really, really happening.*

"I told you, you can't go just yet." He pushes me back onto the bed and points toward the corner. "I have a camera there, so I'll be able to see and hear if you need anything."

"A camera?" I study the small, round ball in the far corner, mesmerized by its blinking red light. "If I need anything? What are you talking about?"

"It's how I knew you were awake." He seems almost proud of himself. As if he's done me a favor.

"You've been...watching me?" The hair on the back of my neck stands on end.

"Just to make sure you were okay. I want to keep you safe." He smiles, touching my arm as if it's meant to be reassuring.

"I appreciate that, but I should really get going and try to see a doctor to make sure everything's okay. Passing out isn't normal for me." *At least not when I'm sober.* "If you want to make sure I'm okay, you should let me go now so I can get checked out by a professional." I fight for my voice to sound more powerful than I feel.

"I'm sorry, Mari. Truly." His face tilts toward the floor, then back up at me. "But I'm afraid that's not possible."

I blink. "What are you talking about? I don't understand what's happening."

"You're going to stay with me for a while. I'm not going to hurt you. I just want to get to know you better."

His grin goes wide. "I want to make sure you're okay because I don't think you are."

Chills line my skin and I suddenly feel dizzy, as if this is all just a fever dream. I can only hope it is. "But why? Why would you do this? This is kidnapping. You can't just hold me here against my will." I hate how badly my voice is shaking. I hate myself for not being strong and assertive, as I know I should be.

"Of course I can. More than that, *I have to*. It's my duty. My obligation. Mari," he says, eyes sparkling, chest puffing, "I'm your number-one fan."

CHAPTER FIVE

W hen the door opens again, it's been several hours since he left. Maybe a day. In here, I have no way of keeping track of time.

The room is in disarray—the DVDs he left me are scattered on the floor, drawers flung out from the nightstand. The lamp is lying on the floor, shade askew, but otherwise still lit. All of this damage is a product of my reaction moments after he left and locked the door, shoving me to the ground so hard I cracked my elbow on the concrete floor. The impact left a nasty bruise.

In some ways, it still doesn't feel real. In some ways, I still want to please him. To be on my best behavior.

In others, I want to slit his throat.

Conveniently, he's left nothing that would make an effective weapon. The drawers are thin, pressed wood that might cause a headache, but little else. The lamp is a cheap plastic meant to look like silver metal. I know this can't be an accident; he's thought everything through. Perhaps I'm not the first person he's locked down here.

He surveys the room with what I suspect is pride in his eyes before laying a change of clothes on the bed. Sweatpants and a T-shirt that must belong to him. The look in his eyes tells me I've done exactly what he hoped I would. Without a single word, he begins cleaning the room. He picks up the drawers and slides both back into the nightstand. He carefully places each pair of fuzzy socks into the top one. When he's done, he sets the bucket from the corner—which I'm assuming will be my makeshift toilet while I'm here—back into place.

The DVDs are next, and he takes the time to place them back in a neat stack, bookending it with both hands to make sure it's straight. He sets the lamp where it belongs and then, with meticulous effort, picks up each individually wrapped candy and places them back in the yellow, plastic bowl before putting it on the nightstand too. Last is the peaches, some of which are no longer any good. He drops the bruised ones into the bucket and dusts off the few that can be saved before putting them in their bowl and back on the dresser, where the stack of DVDs rests. Until now, I haven't thought to ask how I'm supposed to watch any of these DVDs with no television in the room.

Once he's satisfied with his work, he sits on the edge of the bed, running a hand over the comforter to smooth out the space in front of him. I pull my knees into my chest, refusing to meet his eyes.

"Now then, are you calmed down?"

As if I'm a fucking toddler.

"I understand this is all somewhat upsetting, but I assure you I have no plans to harm you. I love you. Don't you see that?"

I don't justify this Annie Wilkes wannabe with an answer.

"Mari, your books have changed my life. Truly. I've read all of them seven times each."

I have no doubt that's an exact figure.

"You have no idea what you mean to me. I... I feel like I've screwed this all up. I just wanted to talk to you. To pick your brain. I don't want you to be afraid of me." He touches my knee gently, and I flinch. "Please talk to me."

I look up at him then, searching his eyes for a shred of humanity. "I want to go home, Owen."

"I know. I know you do." He doesn't say I can. Or will. What if I never do? Before this, I wasn't sure it mattered. Since losing Declan and Liam, nothing mattered. But now... *Now,* I'm positive I want to get out of this room. I want to fight. I want to go home to my own space, live whatever portion of this life I have left. "Is there anything else I can get you to make you more comfortable? Wine, maybe? Or... Are you hungry?"

I am, but I have no intention of eating or drinking anything else he brings me. "Did you drug me?" I ask.

The side of his mouth quirks up a bit.

"You did, didn't you?" I study him. "Are you even Owen Doyle?" He has to be, doesn't he? The email matched his website. His silence gives me the answer I feared. "Who are you?" I demand.

"It doesn't matter. I'm no one. Nothing. I'm just a man. You're... You're everything, Mari. Everything to me. Everything that matters."

"So, you're not a producer? This was all a lie to get me here so you could... *What*, exactly? What is your plan?"

"I'm not a producer, but I'm something better. Your number-one fan, remember? I mean that. I know everything about you that's available to the other readers, but I want to know more. I deserve to know more. I need to get to know the mind behind the characters I've fallen in love with."

"I don't understand. You could've just emailed me. I respond to every—"

"I did. Several times. We've talked so much, Mari." He tilts his head to the side as I run back through the thousands of emails I've responded to over the years. Some creepy, but most polite and well-meaning. Did I have any inkling what sort of monster I was talking to then? "See? You've already forgotten me. To you, I'm just another fan. A number. A face among millions. But I needed more. I needed to *know you* in person. I'm sorry for how it had to happen, and it's my greatest hope that someday, you'll be able to understand that. I also hope, someday, you'll be able to forgive me for it."

I clutch my hands to my chest. "Of course I will. I'll forgive you if you let me go. I'm so happy to meet you. Honestly. I'm sorry I didn't realize we'd spoken. I'm so grateful for your support. But I need to go home. My family will be worried about me."

"Your family is gone, Mari. I know about the shooting. I know you're alone."

Shooting. The word assaults me, slamming into my chest with a vengeance. Most days I can't even bring myself to think about it. Still, occasionally it sneaks up on me, a similar incident on the news or in a movie, and I'm right back in that moment. Reliving every second of the horror.

He lifts his hand, brushing a bit of my hair back from my eyes. "It must've been so hard."

"Don't talk about them," I say through gritted teeth, hating the betraying tears that line my eyes. I hate him so much it physically hurts me.

"Please don't cry. You're not alone anymore, Mari. Don't you get that? You have me now. You'll never be alone again." He pulls me into a hug, whispering gently in my ear as he rocks us back and forth. "It's all going to be okay. I promise everything will be okay." My entire body is stiff as a board under his grip, and I loathe him so much I feel like I could combust.

"What do you want from me?" My lips brush the fabric of his shirt, and I want to vomit at the rancid scent of his sweat. My only hope at this point is that Kassara has called the police with my location. His name will do nothing for me, but still, I'm so grateful I had the forethought to give her the address where I was headed.

It will only be a matter of time before the police arrive and I'm rescued. I have to hold onto that hope.

Seemingly in no hurry to answer my question, he pulls back and lies down on his stomach across the bed, his feet up in the air over his back like we're girlfriends at a picnic discussing the cute boy in class. "I want to talk about your books."

"What about them?"

He clicks his tongue, thinking. "Well, we'll start with *Deadly Games*."

"What do you want to know?" The thought of my debut story reminds me of my husband, of the early days when this was all still just a pipe dream. When we'd sat in the living room of our first apartment and dreamed of what someday might be our reality. That was when I'd had the initial idea for what would become my debut novel. But I refuse to share any of those memories with this monster. Those are mine. They belong to me. They once belonged to us. To the man I loved more than anything else in this world.

"How did you come up with it?"

"I, um, I heard a story on the news about a serial killer who carved a symbol into his victim's skin." Saying it out loud makes me feel terrible, even now. "I thought it would make for an interesting story."

He rolls over to his side, propping his head up on his palm. "Oh, your instincts are so spot on. Interesting, it was. One of the darkest, most twisted books I've ever read. As soon as I finished, I knew you were something special." He stares at me with wide-eyed wonder. "I brought it to class with me because I couldn't put it down." As he says the words, I can see on his face he's revealed more than he meant to. "Anyway, I—"

"You were in college?" He looks my age or older, so

this is surprising but not completely unbelievable. I had just turned thirty when my debut novel was published thirteen years ago.

"I'm a teacher, actually." He stands, approaching the door and walking out without warning. I have no idea what just happened.

When he returns moments later, he's holding my book. The pages are marked with multicolored tabs. Nearly every page has a tab on it, and from the looks of it, some have multiples. He opens it to one of the many tabs, clears his throat, and begins to read.

"*Her flesh is sweet. Unmarred by the tattoos so many women ruin themselves with these days. No stretch marks. No scars. She's beautiful. I can't believe I'm the one who gets to mark her for the first time.*" He puts his hand in his pocket and glances at me. "Do you know what happens next?"

I swallow. Eventually, the killer catches her and kills her, leaving his initials in her skin. But first... "He chases her."

He closes the book, his eyes going dark. "Run, Mari."

CHAPTER SIX

In the small room, there's nowhere to run. But, at the command, he tosses the book and launches himself forward. I leap from the bed, crying out as I grab the lamp and throw it behind me, toward him. It bounces off his chest and slams on the floor. This time, the light flashes, then goes out. I'm suddenly very thankful for the dim overhead light I turned on after waking up. The idea of being alone with this monster in the dark is enough to make me dizzy.

I dart across the room, turning my back to him in front of the camera. "Please, Owen." I don't know what to call him. Owen isn't his name, but there's nothing else. Not-Owen, perhaps. "*Please.* You don't want to do this." I sidestep as he lunges for me, then dart for the bed and step up onto the mattress. As I take another step, the blanket twists around my ankle, tripping me, and I feel his hand grasp my thigh. I fall, kicking, and my foot connects with something. He groans, and when I look back, I see blood dripping from his upper lip. He wipes the back of his hand across it, grinning as I try to right myself and get onto my feet. "You said you wouldn't hurt me. If you care about me, you wouldn't do this."

I fall off the bed and to the ground and crawl forward, feeling like a woman in a horror movie and hating myself for not behaving better. I should be smarter than this. Stronger. Braver than this.

"It's because I care that I *must* do this, Mari. Soon, you'll understand." He towers over me, walking in my direction slowly. I grab the nightstand and haul it forward to the floor, creating a small barricade between us, but he steps over it with ease. I scramble to my feet and move farther away until my back is against the door, and I'm stuck. I've backed myself into a literal corner. He takes hold of my waist, and I become deadweight in his arms, hoping he'll drop me. Instead, he tightens his grip, fighting to keep me upright.

I wish I'd taken a self-defense course.

I wish I'd paid more attention to the action films Declan loved so much.

I wish I'd never come here.

I wish I'd never opened that email.

I flail and throw punches and kick and scratch, connecting with more than I miss, but he seems entirely unfazed. It's as if he can't feel what I'm doing to him at all.

I throw another punch and he releases my body without warning.

CRACK.

My head connects with the floor with too much force. My eyes instantly blur with tears. The sound, or perhaps my reaction to it, snaps him out of his trance.

The darkness in his eyes disappears as he steps back, dropping to the ground in front of me. "Are you okay?"

"*Am I...okay?*" I spit out, completely out of breath and stunned at the look of concern on his face. "You just...tried to attack me." I put my hand to my scalp, searching for blood. Thankfully, I don't feel any.

"We were playing a game," he says simply. "Acting out your book. I thought you knew."

"Please"—I struggle to sit up—"I need to go home."

He chuckles like I'm joking. "Don't be silly."

"This isn't a joke. What you're doing is a crime. You can't keep me here."

Ignoring me, he stands and lifts me up over his shoulder, carrying me to the bed. I should fight, but I'm afraid doing so will only restart the game.

He kisses my forehead, leaving a dot of saliva on my skin. "I'll be right back."

He leaves the room, and I touch the back of my head again, an aching pain growing at the base of my skull. I hear the click of a lock that tells me he's locked me in from the outside.

My elbow stings, and I realize I burned it on the carpet. With him gone, I take the time to check myself for other injuries now that my adrenaline is waning.

A bruise is already forming on my hip where I nicked something, but other than that, I'm relatively okay.

At least, as okay as you can be while being held captive by a nameless fan.

How could I have ever been stupid enough to believe his lies? Why did I think anything so amazing could happen to me? I haven't written, released, or promoted in a year. I'm barely alive—a shell of who I used to be. I don't leave my house. Don't see my old friends. I don't even enjoy reading anymore. I sit on the couch, or in bed, watch television, and drink until I fall asleep. My life is unrecognizable from two years ago. Why on earth would I think something so good could happen now? Why did I think I deserve anything good?

And what the hell is taking Kassara so long with the cops?

It has to at least have been a day since I arrived here. She was supposed to call the police if I didn't reach out when I left that night. I know I told her—twice—that everything was okay, but surely by now she's realized it very much isn't.

When Not-Owen reappears, he's holding a silicone wineglass that reads **I'm the fun grandma.** He holds it out, and when I don't take it, he places it on the end table. "Chardonnay," he reminds me. I hate the way my throat begs for it, like we aren't in a bit of a situation here. Like there aren't more pressing concerns. "Your favorite."

I hate that he knows me so well. Hate that I've made myself so open and available online to anyone who cares to look. Hate that I did it all for the sake of a career I no longer care about because someone somewhere told me it was the only way to reach readers, to make a name for myself, to be someone.

"Are you okay? Is there anything else I can get you? I want you to be comfortable here, Mari. It's important to me."

I refuse to answer, grinding my teeth together until my jaw hurts.

"Suit yourself," he says eventually, just before he turns to leave. When he does, I eye the wineglass. It's likely drugged, yet somehow it's still tempting. Alone, wounded, and scared, whatever's in this drink is the least terrifying part of my new reality.

I lift it and sling the glass across the room, refusing to buy into his games.

Then, I lay my head on the pillow and think of Declan and Liam. Dec would know what to do if he were here. I listen closely, waiting to hear their voices as I always do while I fall asleep. When they don't come, when I realize how completely and utterly alone I am, tears begin to fall, and I wish more than anything else to wake up from this nightmare.

CHAPTER SEVEN

—————

Several hours pass before I see Not-Owen—or whatever his name is—again. At least a day, I think, but probably more.

By the time he returns, my body is trembling with pain from the lack of alcohol and food. I've licked up the droplets of wine from the wall and carpet, but there wasn't enough to matter. Not enough to stop the withdrawals. I've eaten all six of the peaches he left for me and several of the LifeSavers. Still, it's not enough. My stomach feels as if it's caving in on itself, crying out for anything of substance. I curse myself for not having the foresight to eat before I arrived, but I'd anticipated a meal, and nerves had prevented me from even snacking.

Now, my body burns from lack of nutrients. Which is why, when he appears in the doorway holding a tray of food and another silicone glass of wine, I resign myself to the fact that I don't care if it's drugged or not.

I'm too hungry.

I sit up, eyeing the tray, my mouth practically watering. There's a peanut butter and jelly sandwich—thank goodness I don't have any allergies, but then again, my *number-one fan* probably knows that—and a handful of baby carrots on a small plate, plus two clear, silicone glasses—one of wine, the other of water. Not iced.

Not exactly a five-star meal, but it will do.

He lowers the tray onto the bed and eyes the wineglass on the floor with a wry smile. I don't wait for permission or assurance this meal won't poison me. Instead, I grab the glass of wine and guzzle it down. It's gone in two gulps. When I'm done, I read the writing on the front. **I don't give a sip. I'm retired.**

I grab the sandwich and inhale the scent. The sweet, grape jelly and peanut butter between pillowy-soft slices of bread fill my mouth as I take the first bite. The groan I release is involuntary.

Despite my attempts to make it last, the sandwich is gone in four bites, and I wipe the corners of my mouth with my fingers, popping the remnants of peanut butter and jelly onto my tongue and licking them clean. Next, I grab the carrots and chomp on them more slowly, my hunger slightly satiated.

All the while, this man watches me without saying a word. As if I'm a zoo exhibit. I half expect him to start taking notes or to pull out his phone and snap photographs to put on whatever creepy Marietta Morgan blog he's undoubtedly in charge of.

Watch Mari eat—see how she chews! Does she prefer strawberry or grape jelly? Find out now!

When I'm done, when every crumb has been cleaned from the plate piece by piece, I take the water. "Thank you," I say softly. Perhaps it's my deeply ingrained manners, or the fact that I'm hoping if I'm polite, he won't hurt me anymore. Either way, I want to be kind to him. And I hate myself for it.

He sits down on the bed, placing the empty tray on the floor. "How are you feeling?"

I stare at him, not understanding how he expects me to answer.

"Does your head still hurt?"

"I'm okay," I say finally. "Still hungry." I eye the tray on the floor. "Could I have more?" I hate how pathetic I sound, despise the fact that I have to ask him for anything.

"Soon." He reaches down and picks up the wineglass I tossed on the ground before, setting it on the tray. "You didn't drink this."

It's not a question, but I shake my head anyway.

"I'm proud of you," he says, releasing a long breath. "You have to quit drinking so much if you want to be able to write."

"How would you know how much I drink?" I demand.

He folds his hands together in his lap. "You get shipments of alcohol sent to your house weekly. It used to be only monthly."

I eye him, feeling as if I've been stripped naked right here. "You've been stalking me?"

He nods, unashamed. "Watching you, yes. So I knew what you needed from me."

"You've been to my house?"

"On occasion."

"Enough to know I get shipments weekly." *Sometimes twice a week*, but I don't mention that.

"I wanted to make sure you were okay. And I saw that you weren't." He looks down. "It got worse and worse. *You* got worse. Your drinking has become out of control ever since..." Tactfully, he trails off.

"Yeah," I say bitterly. "Well, you lose your family and let me know if it doesn't drive you to drink."

He scoffs, muttering, "I'd have to have a family first."

Seeing an in, I pry, "Why don't you?"

His eyes meet mine, and he suddenly looks sheepish. "I've never been with anyone seriously. It's...just never worked out."

Well, why the hell not? You seem totally normal, Not-Owen. I put on a fake look of concern. "I don't believe that. I'm sure, if you put yourself out there, you could meet a nice woman, er, a nice person and start a family."

His eyes flick down to my lips, and ice fills my stomach. "Maybe someday."

I force a smile and look down.

"It's been more than a year since you released a

book," he says, back to business. "What's your new one about?"

"I haven't been writing," I admit. "Not yet. But as soon as I get home, I will. I was actually planning to start my new one in November. Fall always helps me get into a mood for writing."

"Excellent. Keeping you here with me will be helpful then. I can make sure you don't drink more than what's necessary. Keep your head clear. Help you with story ideas even. Maybe you could name a character after me."

"How can I name a character after you if I don't know your name?" I ask.

He twists his lips. "You will soon. Once I know I can trust you."

I swallow, picking at a piece of skin near my thumbnail.

"Would you do that?" he asks after a beat. "Name a character after me, I mean. I'll be a reason for your success, after all. I sort of already am. I probably own more copies than anyone else in the world. And now, I'm going to get you back on track. You'll owe me, but I'd never collect on it. I want you to know that, Mari. All I want is for you to get back to doing what you love. Telling me stories."

Ignoring his question, I say, "I...I don't know if I can do that—if I can tell stories—without drinking. I do my best writing when I drink." He gives me a challenging look, but I don't shrink away. "I do. Always have. I've mentioned it in interviews before. Surely you knew that."

His lips press together, and for a brief moment, I

worry I've overstepped. Or, worse, that he'll sniff out my lie. "I must've missed it. Either way, maybe things need to change. You haven't been writing, and you're drinking more than ever. Why's that?"

"Because I've been sad," I say simply.

His upper lip curls. "We both know that's not why. You can't write if you're drunk. But, thankfully, I'm going to help with that. We're going to get you sober." Suddenly, my mouth is a desert. The Sahara. An arid wasteland.

"*What? Seriously?*" Somehow, I'm more upset over this news than being locked in here. Something is seriously wrong with me.

"I'm going to fix you, Mari. Don't worry." He pets my head, his palm sliding down my cheek as he practically reads my mind. "It's all going to be okay now."

"You're the one bringing me alcohol now," I say, instantly regretting the words because I don't want him to stop. "How is that fixing me?"

"I will bring you two glasses of wine a day. Enough to make sure you don't go into withdrawal, enough to make sure you don't die. But not enough to sustain the nasty habit you've picked up."

I swallow, the wine seeming to sour in my stomach. I wish I'd made it last longer.

He stands, lifting the tray from the floor, and exits the room. Moments later, he returns carrying a stack of my books. He tosses them onto the bed. "Here."

I gesture toward them as if they were garbage. That's what they feel like most days. I don't want anything to do with the woman who wrote these books. "What am I supposed to do with these?"

I don't want to touch them or think about them. They're littered with too many painful memories. The book I was writing when Liam went to kindergarten. The book whose signing caused me to miss his championship soccer game. The books I read aloud to Declan as I wrote them, quizzing him endlessly about a character's believability and his guesses on the plot twists. I don't want to relive any of that. I can't. I won't survive it.

"Find your inspiration again."

With that, he's out of the room, and I hear the faint click of the lock.

Once again, I'm alone.

CHAPTER EIGHT

For a while, I simply stare at the haphazard pile of books at the end of the bed. I want to kick them to the floor, but I'm afraid of doing anything that might damage them for his sake.

It strikes me as funny. They're my words. Stories that once existed in my head alone, yet he cares about them more than I do. At least, more than I do now. Once you've lost the two people who matter most to you in the world, no other loss or pain can compare.

It's why I'm struggling to write now. Either I write something truly horrific, something that feels worthy of the grief and shock and loss I've experienced, or I write watered-down garbage that will only hurt, anger, or otherwise cause pain to the readers who've experienced no true loss of their own.

The readers who don't know what true pain is.

Both options feel cheap.

Hesitantly, I pick up my debut novel and run a hand

over the cover. I remember the day I first saw it. I was in a meeting for work when the email came in, and I'd gasped so loudly that everyone at the table turned to look at me. My district manager knew about the book deal and was thankfully understanding of my excitement, but I had to leave and call Declan right away.

When I came home, he had a bottle of wine and takeout from my favorite restaurant waiting for me. I'll never forget the way his arms wrapped around my waist and how he twirled me around the room, saying over and over again how proud he was.

I couldn't have written a better reaction for him. It was everything.

He was everything.

I open the cover and read the dedication, tears brimming my eyes.

To Declan, my first reader, my greatest love, and my biggest supporter—
Thank you for being here. Thank you for being mine.

It hurts. It all just hurts.

I turn the page to chapter one, knowing all the hope that went into this page. It radiates it for me—the hope, the pure joy, the promise of things to come. When I first wrote these words, I had no idea what my life would become. I had no idea if any of this would work out or if I'd even ever finish the book. It was simply a dream. A story in my head and the belief of the man that I loved more than life behind me.

In those days, it was just us, and we were just trying to make it happen. Every day after work, after Liam was down for the night, I'd sit in the makeshift office we'd set up in the corner of the living room and tell myself a story, hoping one day someone else might read it.

Now, I hold in my hand the proof that they did. The proof that my dream came true.

And look where it got me.

I'd trade all of this to have them back. Every second, every ounce of happiness, if it would bring them back to me.

Slowly, unwillingly, I begin to read.

I'VE REACHED chapter thirteen by the time the door opens again, and he appears with more food. This time, it's a turkey sandwich and a handful of cherry tomatoes and sliced cucumbers. He sets it down on the dresser, regarding the book in my hand with a smug grin as he gathers my dirty clothes from the floor. I hate that I'm wearing anything that belongs to him, but I can't deny how good it feels to have changed out of my outfit and into something comfortable. I'm scared to ask what he'll do with the clothes he's taking from me, though I'm nearly positive I'll never see them again.

"You're reading."

I close the book and toss it aside. "Yeah, well, I finished up all my errands and had some spare time."

"It's good for you," he says, ignoring my sarcasm. "I know you must think I'm being cruel, but you love writing, Mari. I can't let you waste that talent. It wouldn't be fair to the rest of us."

He places the pile of clothes on top of the dresser before passing me the tray. I dig into my meal, shoveling the food into my mouth as fast as I can. I glance at the bucket as the urge to use it hits me. Up until now, I've managed to avoid it, but I won't be able to for much longer.

"When are you going to let me out of here?" I ask, wiping the corner of my mouth with the back of my hand.

He looks away, easing down onto the edge of the bed. "I don't know. I'll keep you posted."

"You're going to, though, right? You're going to let me go?"

His face hardens as he snaps back to look at me. "Am I so hard to be around that you're already counting down until you can leave me? Is that it, Mari? Haven't I taken good care of you? Haven't I made sure you have everything you need?"

"Of course," I mutter. "You've been so kind to me, O —" I pause. "What should I call you?"

He doesn't answer. "How do you feel reading your stories again?"

"I... It's interesting. Hard. My stories are pieces of my life. My history. It's hard to relive some of it."

He nods. "Because of what happened to them?"

"Yes. And other things." I point to my third novel. "My dad died while I was writing this one. And we lost our dog when I was on tour for this one." I point to the fifth.

"I understand that. Your books are points in my life, too. I can tell you what was going on in my life when I read each one." The skin around his eyes wrinkles with joy. "That's why you're special, Mari. Why your books mean so much to your readers. To *me*. I had no one in my life. My parents never wanted anything to do with me. I had no friends. No girlfriends. It was only books. And movies. They helped me escape. Your books saved my life when I was at my lowest point. When I thought I couldn't go on. I know you don't agree with my methods, but that's why I had to do this. I... I know how this sounds, but I believe, *no*, I know... Your books saved me, so I could save you."

"I don't need saving," I say, shaking my head slowly. I study him, hoping with everything in me that I can make him understand. "Truly. I lost my family. I'm grieving. It's normal. I'm allowed to be sad."

"It's been a year. It's time to put yourself back together. Be sad, sure, but if you don't start writing now, you never will."

"Maybe that's okay."

"*No.*" He bellows the word as if transformed into a monster. My eyes are so wide it hurts to stare at him, my breath caught in my throat. He stands, his arm rearing back, and he slaps the tray of food across the room. The contents of the sandwich separate, and the tomatoes and cucumbers slam into the wall and bounce off, landing on the carpet. "No. That will *never* be okay. Do you hear me? *Never.*" He's shaking, fuming. His face splotches with scarlet. "You have to keep going, Mari. If not for yourself, for us."

"There are other authors—"

"*Other* authors?" He scoffs, chuckling under his breath dryly. "I can't believe you just said that. It's like I don't know who you are anymore. Like you don't know who you are." He grabs the buttons of his shirt, working them angrily until it's open.

He glances down and I stare in horror at what he's trying to show me. My words have been inked into his skin, all across his chest, his stomach, his arms. There seems to be no rhyme or reason, no pattern, but I recognize my words. Lines I once spent countless hours perfecting. *My words are tattooed into his skin.* It takes several seconds for me to process the realization. I suddenly feel as if I might get sick. "There are no other authors who compare to you. None who make me feel as seen as you do. Don't you get that?"

"I'm sorry," I tell him. I can't bear to meet his eyes. This just keeps getting worse. Every time I think there's nowhere more troubling to go, he manages to prove me wrong. "I didn't understand, but I do now. I'm sorry."

Clearly disgusted, he stalks out of the room and locks it behind him, leaving the food on the floor for me to finish.

Without shame, I slip off the bed and begin gathering

tomatoes and cucumbers back onto the plate, then piece the sandwich together again. I don't feel hungry now, but I have no doubts my appetite will return.

I don't expect him to come back in, so when the door opens again, I scramble back to the bed in a hurry.

He sticks his head inside and looks at me. The darkness I saw in his eyes before is back, and it chills me to my core. He steps into the room and closes the door, slipping the key into the dead bolt to lock us in from the inside. I've never seen him take so many precautions.

When he turns around, he shoves his hand into his pocket and retrieves a knife.

"What are you doing?"

He reaches for my third novel, his Adam's apple bobbing as he swallows, and without saying a single word, he's given me an answer.

Soon, both people in this room will have my words carved into their skin.

CHAPTER NINE

"With her sedated, there will be less of a struggle. Not quite as fun for me, but less risk. After the last time, I've decided to mitigate my risks whenever I can." He reads from my book with wild, crazed eyes, twirling the knife in his hand.

"Please. You don't have to do this," I say.

The only sign he's heard me is that his voice gets louder. "I open the knife." As he reads the words, he opens the pocketknife in his hands. My body is made of solid ice as I scan the room, searching for a weapon I may have overlooked before.

"Please, Owen," I cry. "Please don't do this. You haven't hurt me yet. If you cross that line, this all becomes so much worse. Please, just... Please, don't."

"Lowering myself over her, I take hold of her ankle. The skin is so smooth, it's almost a crime to mar it. Almost." He takes hold of my ankle, jerking me across the bed toward him. I kick my free foot, my heel jabbing into his stomach. He doubles over, but he doesn't miss a beat as he tosses the book down, reciting the words from memory over my struggle. "*I lower the blade to her skin.*"

I can hardly hear him through my screaming, which is beginning to sound animalistic. He wouldn't actually do this, would he? He can't. It's barbaric. It's insane. It's disgusting.

He's obsessive. Delusional maybe, but I need to believe he's not a monster...

I kick his stomach again and again, but he's hardly fazed, swatting away my legs when they aim for him each time. He climbs onto the bed, straddling my waist with his body facing my feet. I pound my fists into the bed, rolling and squirming and screaming until my voice gives out. I can't hear him reciting the words I once wrote anymore, but I know he is.

Then suddenly, it all stops.

I feel the blade slice my skin with a single, fluid motion. Everything in me turns to fire. I'm being scorched by lightning from the inside. Bile rises in my throat as I feel the blade slice into my skin again, and I barely turn over in time to vomit onto the comforter. My body is numb and yet somehow, in such excruciating pain. I feel as if I'm being burned by a white-hot poker. He's practically masterful in the way he slides the knife across my skin, and when he's done, I'm out of energy to fight. He stands, admiring his handiwork, and I lie still, my skin coated in sweat, chest heaving with fast, ragged breaths.

I can't move. Can't think.

I feel empty and weak.

What a terrible fate to have written for myself.

I don't move when he leaves the room except to glance down at the initials he's carved there. *CP*. Blood pours from the wounds—thick, sticky red liquid oozing out across my skin and onto the blue comforter below me.

He returns moments later with a medical kit, his eyes no longer dark and creepy. Suddenly, he's normal. He works diligently from the foot of the bed, pouring liquid over the wound. If it stings, I don't register it, but I smell the sharp hint of alcohol in the air.

He bandages it with care, taping it to my skin and smoothing his hands over the gauze.

"It's going to be okay," he promises. "You just needed to remember what it felt like back then. When you were in your stories. I have to bring you back there." He kisses the wound, but I don't have the strength to kick him in the face like I so desperately want to. "I don't want to be the one to do it, but I have to." He stands, dusting off his knees. "I'll be back with some wine. You deserve it after that."

He leaves, and I feel my adrenaline crashing. My body begins to shake with sobs I can't feel. I can't breathe. My heart is beating too fast.

This is what a panic attack feels like for me. I've had them before, not often but enough. The worst one was when I got the call. When they told me what had happened. When they told me there was a shooter and they couldn't find my husband or my son.

Chills line my body when he returns with another

silicone glass of wine. This one says **Drink your wine. We have crafts to do.**

He pulls me from the bed and eases me onto the hard floor, making quick work of stripping the comforter from the bed and replacing it with a clean one.

Then he lifts me back up onto the bed and hands me two pills from his pocket. "For the pain."

I don't ask what they are or what they'll do to me. This time, when he leaves the room, I swallow the pills and suck down the wine, hearing their voices again as I drift off to sleep within minutes.

CHAPTER TEN

The next time he comes to my room, I'm lying on the end of the bed reading the back cover of *The Faculty*'s DVD case for the hundredth time. I practically have it memorized at this point, but there's quite literally nothing else to do in this space.

I understand now why people lose their minds when left alone for too long, particularly when your mind isn't a safe space to begin with.

I sit up, watching as he walks into the room and locks the door with his key before approaching the bed. I didn't realize I was cold until he hands me a bowl of steaming oatmeal. He's also brought a bottle of room temperature water and my glass of wine. Today's glass says **It's not really drinking alone if the dog's home.**

A single sip of the chardonnay sends my insides into a frenzy. So much so that I don't notice when he crosses to the other side of the bed and pulls my leg toward him.

"*Ouch!*" I try, but fail, to jerk away as he rips the bandage back, staring down at the wound with a hard expression.

It's red and weeping—clearly infected. He pulls the bandage the rest of the way off and reaches for the tray, opening the first aid kit and pulling out the trial-size spray bottle of rubbing alcohol.

"This will sting," he warns seconds before spraying it on. He wasn't lying. The pain is white-hot and sharp, demanding every bit of my attention. I place the glass and bowl down and squeeze my hands into tight fists, wincing. He fans the wound until the pain subsides, then takes a bit of antibiotic ointment with his finger and rubs it on the wound. Each time he passes over my skin, it's as if he's cutting me open again.

He swipes his finger on the side of his pants and prepares a new bandage. "How are you feeling?"

"Hungry," I tell him, reaching for the bowl of oatmeal again after taking the smallest sip of wine. I've learned to pace myself in such a short amount of time. "And bored. Can I at least have a TV or something?"

He seems to contemplate it. "Yeah, I can do that. I'll bring down my laptop, and we'll watch something together later. I have to disconnect the Wi-Fi first."

I nod. "Of course." Nothing sounds worse than watching a movie with him, but I don't argue. "Thank yo—"

He cuts me off with his hand held up in the air, shoving the opposite one into his pocket. When he looks at the phone in his hand, he curses under his breath.

"Everything okay?"

He hardly looks at me as he power walks across the room. "Be quiet," he orders just before shutting the door. I take another bite of the oatmeal slowly, no idea what just happened but too hungry to care.

He left the first aid kit here.

The realization slams into me as I swallow the bite down. Placing my bowl back onto the bed, I slide the first aid kit toward me and sort through the contents. Maybe there's a scalpel or needle I can use to...do *something*. To my disappointment but not surprise, it's mostly packs of gauze and antibiotic cream. There are a few latex gloves, bandages of various sizes, an instant cold pack, burn cream, the alcohol spray, and a few antiseptic towelettes. I move two rolls of medical tape and cotton swabs, searching for something. *Anything.*

There's not even a pair of tweezers. If anything sharp existed here before, he's taken them out already. I toss both handfuls of things into the box again and push it back into place.

Then, something strange settles over me.

Did I hear the door lock when he left?

It's become such a part of the routine that I've stopped listening for it, but there's a voice in my head saying I didn't hear it this time. The movement feels unfinished.

Cautiously, I stand from the bed. Despite the fact that I've been making sure to walk laps around the room several times a day to keep up my strength, my legs are tired from not being used. My feet hurt on the cold, hard, carpeted floor. I'm barefoot—as he didn't leave my shoes down here—when I reach the door. Silently, I promise myself that if the door opens, I will run and fight with every ounce of strength I have. That I won't stop running until I'm safe, somewhere far away from him.

That, no matter what, I won't stop, won't hesitate, won't let my fear control me.

With a trembling hand, I twist the doorknob slowly.

It opens.

I pull back, just waiting for a lock to catch, but it doesn't happen. I step out into the space in front of me, a boulder sinking in my chest.

No.

It's impossible...

This is not the house I visited before. Wherever I am, it's not the place I was supposed to meet "Owen," not the address I gave Kassara. Crushing defeat settles in my gut, and I know, without a doubt, I am now the only chance I have of getting out of this place.

All this time, I've been waiting for someone to save me. Waiting for Kassara to finally realize something's wrong and send the police. I've been in denial, convinced she's just been distracted or that the police have been busy, even though I know better.

I didn't want to face the truth, but now I have no choice.

The room outside of mine is cold and dark, and there's a set of rickety stairs in front of me. The lower floor of the house, which I know isn't a basement because I see light through a small window on the far side of the room, is basically empty, with a washer and dryer to my right and a clothesline hung across the room, where various shirts and pants are hanging. As if he's made this bottom floor his closet.

I look back just once, spying the dead bolt and chain on the door of my prison cell from the outside for the first time. With that, I grab hold of the railing and carefully make my way up the staircase.

As I near the top, the sound of his voice sends chills down my spine. "What are you talking about? I told you, I'm fine."

Then there's another voice. A woman's voice.

Someone else is in the house.

"I'm worried about you, Chris. Something's going on. I know it is."

"Stop being paranoid. I'm fine. I've just been busy."

I step onto the landing. Directly to my right is a small galley kitchen. Their voices are coming from somewhere farther into the house. In front of me, just a few feet from the staircase, is a door. Sunlight streams in from outside through a window over the sink, and I'm so close to freedom that I can practically taste it. Fresh air and sunny skies dance on my tongue as I place a hand on the doorknob and take a deep breath.

"Why didn't you answer when I called, then? You were supposed to meet me at Brown Dog."

"I told you, I've been busy. And under the weather. Anyway, I don't have time to—"

I twist the doorknob, and the door pulls open with a sharp *click*. The gust of air that hits me is so clean it makes my eyes water. Wherever their voices are coming from, they've stopped.

I reach for the storm door and push the handle, but it doesn't budge.

No.

No.

No.

Everything that happens next is a blur. I search for the lock keeping this door in place, pushing the lever over and over again as it remains unmoved. In the distance, there is a sudden, loud blaring sound.

Re-re-re-re-re-re!

It drowns out whatever's being said. A door shuts, and the sound stops.

Then footsteps.

He's coming.

Someone's coming.

I finally locate the lock, hidden on the underside of the handle, a tiny button tucked away from sight, and press it. The door unlatches, and I push, but then, before I can take a single step, I'm pulled backward by my hair.

I scream, hoping someone will hear me. The woman, wherever she is. A neighbor. Anyone. He slams the door shut, keeping a tight grip on my hair. With a single shove, he could send me tumbling down the narrow staircase to my death.

Instead, he leads me down the stairs like a dog. I wish I was braver, stronger. I wish I was anything like the women I write about. Anna St. James would've torn her hair from her scalp to get away from him. Jolene Clark would've found a way to shove him down the stairs herself. As for me, I walk as he leads me right back to the room, keeping myself on my tiptoes to prevent as much of the searing pain in my scalp as possible. He shoves me inside the room, and I fall to the floor. He stares at me, his chest puffing with heavy breaths, bottom teeth in full view. He's like a bulldog ready for battle.

"Where am I?" I demand, now that I can focus on something besides the pain.

"Home," he says firmly. "You're home."

"This isn't the place where I met you."

He doesn't respond.

"Whose house was that?"

He squats down so he's level with me, and I scoot away until my back hits the nightstand.

"Whose house did I go to?" I ask again. "Was it really Owen Doyle's?"

"Doesn't matter who it belonged to. What matters is that you're never going back." His eyes darken. "You're never leaving this room. Do you hear me? If you ever try that again..."

"You'll what?"

"I won't go so easy on you next time, Mari. Don't play games with me. Don't test me." He glances at the bandaged wound on my leg, which in the struggle has apparently been torn open. Blood seeps through the gauze, painting it brilliant shades of crimson.

He doesn't have to say anything else. We both know he's won, and I've lost.

With that, he stands and leaves the room.

This time, he doesn't forget to lock it.

CHAPTER ELEVEN

Though I have no way to know for sure, I'm positive several days pass before I see him again. *Chris*, apparently. That's what the woman called him.

My body is drenched in a cool sweat, and my joints ache. I've thrown up the remaining contents of my stomach and can't seem to stop shaking. This is withdrawal. I know it, and I hate it. I hate that it's my fault.

That there's no one else to blame, not even him, for the mess I've gotten myself in.

I understand I'm being punished for what I did. No food and nothing to drink for days. I finished the last of the oatmeal, wine, and water he'd left me with for breakfast what feels like a lifetime ago, and since then, I've slept in what feels like a state of delirium, waking in pain, and passing back out. When I'm awake, I've been sustaining myself on the LifeSavers he left me, but that supply is quickly dwindling. His already too-large clothing is practically swallowing me whole, and it seems to get worse by the day. I'm losing weight, losing my sense of reality. My grasp on time. My desire to make it out of here.

When he appears, almost like a figment of my imagination—a monster under my bed—he stands in front of the door for several minutes, just watching me.

"Your name is Chris?" I ask, my voice soft and conversational, as if maybe he's forgotten what I did. As if we can just move past it and act as if it never happened.

"How do you know that?"

"I..." It was a mistake to bring this up, but I realize it too late. Then, I notice the bag in his hand. "What did you bring me? Dinner?" My stomach growls at the thought.

He drops the bag on the bed and holds out my latest wineglass, which reads **I may be wrong, but I doubt it**. Like a dog with a bone, I dive for it, practically ravenous. I take two large gulps of the wine, barely tasting it, and then reach for the bag. Inside, there are two styrofoam containers. I tear open the top one, my throat growing dry at the sight of the spaghetti.

I search for a fork as he crosses the room, and I notice the bag slung across his shoulder. He sits down on the bed next to me and unzips it. I watch, mouth full, as he reveals a laptop.

"I thought we could watch a movie if you still want to."

I swallow. Normally, the idea of watching a gory horror movie while eating spaghetti would disgust me, but since I'm sure I'll have both containers of food gone before he gets the case for one of the DVDs open, I nod. "Sure."

"Do you have any preferences?" He stands and walks toward the stack of DVDs, running a finger down the spines slowly. When he turns back and notices me eyeing the laptop, he says, "There's no internet, remember? Don't do anything stupid."

There's an edge to his voice that gets the point across.

"Um." I clear my throat. "How about the original *Halloween*?"

"Ah. A classic. Good taste." He taps a finger in the air before sliding the DVD from the stack and carrying it over to the bed. Then, he reaches into the bag and pulls out the second container of spaghetti—apparently for himself.

I stare down at what's left of my food, wishing I'd paced myself more. This portion has done little to satiate my hunger, and my sudden disappointment is painful.

He pops the DVD into the laptop's CD drive and pushes it forward on the bed once it begins playing, so we both have a decent view of the screen.

I wish I could pretend I was at home, curled up on the couch with Kassara, watching this film for the hundredth time and laughing at how unrealistic and cheesy, yet somehow perfect, it is. I wish I could be anywhere but here.

When I lean back against the headboard, his scent hits me. "You smell like burgers," I muse, more to myself than anything. As much as I hate him, I find myself missing human interaction more. I just want to have a conversation with someone other than myself.

"The cafeteria," he explains, shushing me and pointing at the screen.

We eat in silence for a long while. Halfway through the movie, I glance over at him. "Chris?"

His eyes dart toward me. "Yeah?"

"I just want you to know...I'm sorry I tried to escape."

He leans forward and pauses the movie before he looks at me. "I don't want you to hate it here, Mari."

"I know. I just...I wish I didn't have to be trapped in this room. I wish I could be out in the rest of the house. I get so bored down here."

"Trust me, I want that too. But you're safe down here. Protected. I can keep an eye on you. Until we get to know each other better, I don't know that you won't try to escape if I let you out—"

"But I won't!" I promise him. "I swear I won't. If you'll just give me another chance, I—"

He puts a hand on my leg, lips drawn together with wide-eyed sympathy. "Mari, you're not ready for that yet. I'm sorry. You have to stay down here a while longer. Once I know I can trust you, once you actually want to be here with me, maybe then things can change."

"I understand," I lie. The tears in my eyes are real, though. He brushes one away with his thumb, and it takes all my strength not to flinch or bite it off at the knuckle.

"I'm doing this for you, Mari. I know you don't really

understand it, but I love you. I want you to be safe. Healthy. Happy again."

I bite my bottom lip, looking down. "I guess I would feel safer if I could learn more about you."

He gives me a hesitant look. "What do you want to know?"

"Can you tell me where we are?"

He shakes his head, taking another bite of his spaghetti. "We haven't left South Carolina. I'll tell you that much. That's all you need to know."

"And...and you're a teacher?"

He nods. "Correct."

"Will you tell me whose house we were at before? Not this one?"

"No, not this one," he confirms. "But it doesn't matter whose house it was. I only borrowed it so I could meet you." He turns toward me more. "I just want to know you, Mari. Really, really know you. And I want you to know me, too. We're more alike than you think."

"How so?" I press, avoiding the urge to pull away when he scoots a bit closer.

"Well, we both live in Charleston. Do you think that's a coincidence?"

Thousands of other people also live here, but I don't point that out. "No, I suppose not."

"And we both love horror movies. And reading."

"True."

"I know you don't see it yet, but we were meant to meet each other. I believe that. I was meant to find your books and then, someday, to find you." He chuckles to himself. "We're soulmates, Mari. Tried and true. Don't you see that?"

"I do." I look down. "And I know you've taken good care of me. The grape candies, all of my favorite movies. It's like..." I lift my eyes to meet his. "It's like you know me better than anyone else." The lie is heavy and bitter on my tongue. I was known so well by the man I loved. Declan knew everything there was to know about me, from the way I like my tea to the words I needed to hear in every situation. No one could ever compare to the sort of connection we had.

"I know you better than he did?" he asks, reading my mind.

"He?" Of course, we both know whom he's talking about, but I refuse to answer. I can't betray him with that lie, even if he'd never hear it.

"Your husband."

I look away again, running my plastic fork through the spaghetti. "It was just different."

He grabs my arm, his grip too tight. "I know you more than him, Mari. More than anyone. Tell me you know it, too."

His grip tightens, and I send up a silent prayer, *Forgive me, Dec. Please.* "Yes," I squeak. "Of course you do. Better than anyone."

His lips part into a wide grin, and I stare at the green fleck of oregano in between two of his teeth. He leans forward, and before I realize what's happening, his lips meet mine with a hungry kiss.

I pull back—practically leap away, really—and he

stares at me with an expression that sends chills to my core. Pure, unfiltered fury.

"I'm sorry. I just... I haven't been able to brush my teeth down here." The lie comes easily on a shaky breath. I wipe away his kiss slowly. "I'm really sorry, Chris."

"Obviously, you aren't ready yet." He stands, the *yet* in his words a promise this won't be the last time he tries. Then, he closes his laptop, ending the movie early, and stalks out of the room.

When I glance down at the bed, I'm grateful, at least, he's left both containers of spaghetti for me.

CHAPTER TWELVE

The next day when I wake, everything from dinner is gone from where I left it on the floor. The idea that he's been in my room while I sleep is somehow more terrifying than anything else he's done so far.

I sit up, wiping drool from my chin, and look around. It's the first good night of sleep I've had in a while, and at first I thought it was because I'd gone to sleep with my stomach so full, but now I wonder if he slipped something into my food.

When my eyes land on the nightstand, I spot a fresh bottle of water, a new glass of wine, a rose, a toothbrush, and a tube of toothpaste.

My throat goes dry.

Like I suspected, he's not finished with what he started last night.

That's further confirmed when I spot my fourth novel lying on the nightstand beside the lamp. I'd missed it at first.

Chills line my skin as I realize what it means. My fourth novel is about a serial rapist. A man who takes victims into a hidden room in his house, who drugs and assaults and tortures them until he's done with them.

I can't breathe.

Think.

Think.

Think.

I'd tried to be smart last night, tried to connect with him, and this is where it got me. We've probably always been on this path, but now my foolishness has sped up the course.

I glance down at my leg. The bandage is now coated in dried blood. It's been a while since he changed it, but I don't dare wish for him to return. Maybe I'll get blood poisoning and die before he makes it back.

Is that what I want?

I've never been one to actually contemplate suicide, even on my darkest days. But now? This is a fate worse than death. Whatever I've been through is nothing compared to what he obviously has planned for me.

But there's nothing in this room I could use to hurt myself. Nothing sharp. Nothing dangerous.

The tube of toothpaste sits—bright red and distracting—on the nightstand. I pick it up and read the back. Toothpaste is poisonous if you eat enough of it, right?

I remember being so cautious with it when Liam was a young boy. Fluoride. That's the poison. I read the warning label, which says you should contact Poison

Control if you ingest more than the amount necessary to brush your teeth.

Would it be enough to kill me?

It's possible. Of course, it's also possible it will just give me a raging case of the shits or cause me to bleed internally. To prove to him I tried to escape again. To make sure I suffer more. Is it worth the risk?

I wish I could say I'm not serious, but I am. I spend the next several hours contemplating it. Earnestly. Weighing the risks and rewards.

Decision made, I slide to the end of the bed and open the tube.

I drop a pea-sized amount onto the bristles of the toothbrush and brush my teeth carefully, spitting into the bucket Chris must've emptied during his late-night visit.

I'm not going to let him win.

I unequivocally refuse.

I'm not going down without a fight.

CHAPTER THIRTEEN

With my teeth brushed, I feel like a new woman. Like my old self. Granted, my hair is so oily it sticks to my scalp, and I smell worse than I ever have before, but at least it's some piece of normalcy.

I use some of the water he gave me, a pair of fuzzy socks, and the bottom corner of my blanket to try and wash some of the smells off, but I'm not sure it's working. I'm convinced that if the silence doesn't drive me crazy, being filthy will.

What I wouldn't give for a hot bath right now.

Before—before losing them, before that day, before all the bad things, before my world imploded—I used to think a nice soak could solve anything.

When he comes in later that day, I'm attempting to build a house with the DVD cases and the books he's left me. He drops to the floor in front of me. "Did you like my gifts?"

"They were very thoughtful," I say carefully. "Thank you."

"I thought of you when I saw the rose."

I want to ask him where he saw it, where he might've been, but I don't want to press my luck. "Could I ask a favor?" I knock the house down, then stack the DVD cases carefully before standing and placing them back on the dresser.

"Depends on what it is."

"Is there any way I could take a shower?"

He stares at me as if this is an unheard-of concept. "A shower?"

"Yeah. I'm just so dirty down here. It's really starting to bother me. You could lock me inside the bathroom and then bring me right back down when I'm done." My eyes dart back and forth between his, trying to get a read on what he's thinking. "Please, Chris. I just want to feel clean again."

He presses his lips together, looking around the room. "I can't do that, Mari. There are windows in the bathroom, and I don't trust you not to escape. Unless... Unless you want me to be in the room with you."

I swallow. This feels like a test. He doesn't give me long to put in my answer.

"How about this? I'll bring you a bucket of clean water, some soap, and a washcloth so you can clean up. I know it's not exactly a shower, but we can compromise, and I'll meet you in the middle."

I fight against a sigh. He's right. It's better than nothing. "Thank you, Chris." I glance toward the bed. "Is there any way you could change my sheets, too? Or bring me some fresh ones so I could swap them? They're starting to feel gross." Probably another thing for him to sell on his creepy blog.

Marietta Morgan slept on these sheets! You can own Marietta Morgan's sweat! Hair and skin particles included at no additional charge.

He studies the bed. "Yeah, I can do that."

He disappears from the room and returns a few minutes later with a stack of clean sheets and a new comforter. The fresh scent of fabric softener is a welcome surprise in this room, which has started to reek of shit, body odor, stale food, and sweat.

He puts the sheets and comforter down and turns back to me. "Can I trust you not to try anything while I do this?"

There's a tickle at the back of my throat as I answer. "Yes."

"Good." He leans over the bed, tearing back my comforter and sheet, then rips the fitted sheet from the corners, one by one. He tosses them into a pile, and I catch a whiff of my musty smell in the air. As he leans down to put the fresh sheet on the dingy mattress, I decide it's time.

Now or never.

Bracing myself, I wait until he's bent over at the end

of the bed to act. With all of my strength, I shove him forward so his head collides with the wooden footboard. He grabs his forehead, collapsing on the ground.

"*Agh!* What the hell was that for?"

I don't wait. With every ounce of energy I have left in me, I run. I close the door and lock it behind me. I dart up the stairs, knowing he has the key and will be coming right behind me but hoping I've given myself enough of a head start. I reach the back door and turn the lock, pulling it open.

As I reach for the lock on the storm door, I hear him at the bottom of the stairs. He's coming, but I'm faster. I swing open the storm door and pull the main door closed.

Still moving, I take in my surroundings. Everywhere I look, I'm enveloped by fields. There's nothing else.

Nowhere to go.

Nothing to do.

A green, rusting car sits in the driveway, but I have no keys and no idea how to hot-wire vehicles. I should've looked for a key, but I didn't have time. I still don't. I have to figure out what I'm doing right now. I look left and right, trying to decide which way I should run. My bare feet burn on the gravel driveway as I race forward, realizing the fields are my best option.

"Mari?"

Stupidly, I turn toward the sound, startled by how close he is and regretting it in an instant. He's right there. Right behind me.

I waver, releasing a scream as I feel the ice tear through my stomach.

White-hot ice.

Unexplainable.

Unbelievable.

It's pain like I've never felt before.

When I look down, I see the blood. I'm suddenly lightheaded.

My knees give out.

I am too weak for this. I should never have tried to run.

He stares at me completely stone-faced, in no hurry to get us back inside. There's no one around to see what he's done anyway.

No one around to help. To save me.

I drop to my knees, resting against my heels as my head grows fuzzy. Glancing down, I stare in horror as blood pools from my wound. My hands go to the kitchen knife sticking out of my stomach. "Why?" I cry, but I know the answer. I made a choice, and I lost.

He rears a fist back, lips tight. I know the punch is coming seconds before it connects with my temple. Then it all goes black.

CHAPTER FOURTEEN

"You shouldn't have done it. Why did you do it? You never listen. I warned you. I warned you what would happen." The voice is garbled. Distant. I can hardly hear what he's saying. I can't focus on anything but the pain. Pain in my stomach, in my face. Opening my eyes sends a shot of lightning through my muscles. "You shouldn't have done it, Mari. Why did you do it?"

It takes me a few minutes to understand where I am and who the man in front of me is. Why he looks so angry. Why he's pacing at the end of the bed.

Then, all at once, it comes back to me. The reason for my pain.

"*You stabbed me!*" I cry, my voice rough in my throat. I scoot back on the bed, away from where he stands. "You... You *punched* me." I lift a hand to my eye, then lift my shirt to examine the wound. Even the tears forming are painful. Apparently, while I was unconscious, Chris bandaged my wound, though the skin around the gauze and medical tape is already varying shades of reds, purples, and blues. Shouldn't I be in the hospital? Will I die if I don't go? Is that what I want to happen? Is it what *he* wants to happen?

"Yeah, I did, Mari. I had to. You left me no choice. You didn't learn. You never learn. You said I could trust you, and then you betrayed me as soon as you had the chance." The way he's looking at me, it's as if *I* stabbed *him*. He drops to his knees at the edge of the bed, pleading with me. "Don't you understand how much this kills me? I never wanted to hurt you, Mari. I wanted to help you. To help you heal from your loss. To bring you back to the thing you love. Writing. Creating stories for us. For me. But what choice did I have? You were going to run." He lifts a hand to his head, where I notice a gash along his hairline. "And don't forget, you hurt me first."

He lifts a hand to my chin, trying to tip my face up toward his, and I jerk away.

"You're special, Mari. You're very, very special. And I..." His voice catches, and he stands, clutching his hands in front of his stomach. "I love you. I don't know why you can't see that. You're everything to me. And until you'll stay willingly, you'll remain down here. Until I can trust you, I have to keep punishing you."

My eyes flick up to meet his. "What do you mean?"

He reaches for the nightstand, picking up the book he left for me this morning. At least, I'm assuming it's still the last day I remember. I have no way of knowing, really. The pain feels fresh, though. At least within the last few hours. No more than a day.

"Please, Chris..."

The corner of his mouth upturns. "I didn't want to have to do this. Just remember that. Any pain I cause you, anything I have to do now, is your fault."

I pull my knees into my chest, ignoring the agony coursing through me at this moment. It's about to get so much worse.

He opens the book, flipping to a page he clearly has memorized, and begins to read, "*I've never been one for smoking. Never had a taste for it. But now, here, the moment calls for it. I light the cigarette and hold it out. She shakes her head, denies me. It's funny she still thinks she has any control here. She'll learn eventually, though. She'll have no choice. For now, I have to break her. I have to break her in the only way I know how. In the way my parents broke me. It has to hurt. I pull her to me, straddling her on the bed, and grab hold of the collar of her shirt. She struggles against me, terrified whimpers escaping her throat, but she already knows if she screams, it will be worse. She's learning. I resist the urge to stroke her hair, call her a good girl. Now isn't the time for such sentiments, even if I mean them. Pulling the collar of her shirt down, I move the cigarette toward her nearly perfect skin. There are freckles there I hadn't noticed before. A smattering of them across her collarbone. A perfect map for me to follow.*"

He drops the book, and I understand what's happening. I see the parallels in the story. If I fight, it will be so much worse.

"Do you have freckles, Mari?" One side of his mouth upturns, the rest of his face completely still.

"You don't have to do this, Chris. I won't ever, ever hurt you again. I'm so sorry."

He's not listening. There's nothing I can say that will stop this. I'm wasting my breath.

I squeeze my eyes shut, bracing myself for the fate I wrote years ago, as he begins to recite my words from memory.

"*I lower the cigarette to the first freckle, and the scream she releases is pure sin. A wave of pleasure courses through me.*" He lowers the cigarette to my skin as he says the words, and I try my hardest not to cry. The pain is red hot, but over quickly, replaced by something similar to a terrible sunburn.

Again.

Again.

Again.

He traces the pattern of imaginary freckles on my collarbone until I'll sport similar scars to the victim I wrote about, a woman named Noelle, if I'm remembering right.

When he's done, my skin feels as if every layer has been ripped off, exposing tendons, muscles, and raw flesh. My throat is sore from screams I could no longer contain. He stubs the cigarette out on the nightstand and climbs off the bed, clicking his tongue.

"Smoking is a terrible habit, Mari."

I want to look down at the damage he's done, but I don't dare.

"So is lying."

I nod. "I'm sorry."

"Not as sorry as you're going to be."

I eye him.

"Do you remember what happens next?"

I swallow, because I do. Not the rape. Not yet. First comes...

He pulls a pair of pliers from his pocket, a wide grin forming on his lips. "Open wide."

CHAPTER FIFTEEN

"Chris, please. *Please.*" I back away from him, covering my mouth, sheer terror swimming through me and paralyzing me from moving farther when I hit the headboard. "You can't do this. There's no going back from this."

"If you don't want this stuff to happen, why do you write about it?" he demands, staring at me with wild eyes.

"It's just fiction. It's made up. It's just supposed to be a story."

"It's so much more than that, Mari. We both know it. There's beauty in it. In pain. In suffering. In fear." He inches closer, like something out of a horror movie. In the book, the killer plucks out his victim's two front teeth. "You saw that. You got it, more than anyone else. You understand how beautiful pain can be."

Like most people, I'm not the biggest fan of my teeth in general. They could be whiter. My front left one has the smallest chip in it, and I always wished they were more square than rounded, but now, the idea of this is worse than anything else.

How could I have ever written something so horrible without feeling this fear, without living what my characters were living?

"*Please.* I get it. You've taught me. I understand now. I really, really do." I inch toward the edge of the bed, away from him, with a hand held in the air and the other shielding my mouth, begging him to stop this. "I'll do whatever you want, Chris. I'll never try to leave again. I promise. I swear. You've made your point. Just stop!"

He launches himself forward, charging over the bed, and my scream dies in my throat when he grabs my chin and shoves me into the wall, pliers at the ready. I close my eyes, my head digging into the wall behind me, bracing myself for what's to come.

"*Chris?*" The voice startles us both, and he turns around as if he expects her to be standing in the room. The stairs creak, and I hear the sound of someone's footsteps on them. "Are you down here?"

He turns back to me, his eyes black and empty. He puts his finger to his lips, whispering. "If you make a sound, I'll kill you both."

My stomach clenches. I have no doubt he's telling the truth as he shoves the pliers back into his pocket and crosses the room quickly, opening the door and walking back outside.

"What are you doing here?"

I don't know whether I should risk it, but I consider it thoroughly. If she's the only person who could help me, would she be able to get to safety and call for help? Or would he overpower her in a second and make good on his promise by killing us both? And, more than that, what if she doesn't want to help me at all? What if she already knows I'm here and doesn't care? What if, even if she doesn't, she would choose him? Then he'd definitely kill me for not following his rules.

"I wanted to see if you had plans for lunch. I thought I heard someone down here screaming."

"I was watching a movie. Anyway, I've told you to stop dropping by unannounced. I'm busy," he says firmly.

"Busy? You were watching a movie," she points out. My heart pounds against my rib cage. Silently, I beg her to ask more questions. To demand to see what movie he was watching. To know why the screams sounded so realistic, why he's so out of breath.

"You should've called."

She sighs. "Why? You never answer anymore. You're always busy lately. I miss you."

Their voices get softer as I hear the creaks on the stairs telling me they're making their way back up. When I can no longer hear them, I realize he didn't lock the door again.

Not that he forgot, I'm sure, just that he couldn't without making himself look suspicious. I ease toward the door, taking hold of the doorknob. I have to make it out this time. No matter how much pain I'm in. No matter how much I'm hurting. I glance down at the bandaged wound on my stomach.

Last time he caught me, he spared my life, but it

would've been all too easy for him to kill me. If I stay in this room any longer, I'm scared of what my fate will be.

I can't be caught this time.

I pull open the door and step out into the empty room. This time, I need to find shoes. Not having them last time slowed me down on the hot gravel far too much. I search around, spying a pair of black rain boots next to the washer.

I cross the room and slip them on, trying not to think about Chris's feet being in the boots and how unsanitary my lack of socks is. None of that matters right now. I take careful, quiet footsteps toward the staircase, and just as I reach the bottom, I hear that familiar sound: *re-re-re-re-re-re-re*. It cuts off when the house shakes as the door is slammed closed.

He's coming back.

His footsteps are loud on the floor just above my head. Thinking quickly, I dart back across the room and shut the bedroom door without a sound. I have mere seconds to spare as his feet come into view. I dart behind the clothesline, hiding out of view behind a corner section of the wall.

He's whistling as he reaches the door and steps inside, expecting to find me right where he left me. I rush forward, slamming the door shut behind him and locking it, both with the dead bolt and the chain this time.

"What the hell?" He slams a fist into the metal of the door. "Mari, don't do this!"

I ignore him, smiling to myself. With all the speed

and strength I can muster, I rush up the stairs, no longer caring about the sound my shoes are making.

Thud.

Thud.

Thud.

Thud.

I reach the top of the stairs, my heart pounding in my ears as I begin working the multitude of locks.

CRASH.

Downstairs, the door is ripped open, and I hear him fighting with the chain. He releases a growl so loud it feels like it crawls over my skin.

I don't have time.

I pull open the door just as I hear the ominous roar followed by footsteps heading in my direction that lets me know he's torn the chain off the door. If I run out of the storm door now, there's no doubt he'll catch me. There's too much open space beyond this door and nowhere to hide. I need more of a headstart than I've given myself. I really thought the chain would hold for longer than it did.

Thinking quickly, I unlatch the storm door and slam the main door closed.

Then, I slip out of the boots, picking them up and carrying them as I pass through the kitchen. I just need to find somewhere to hide while he looks for me outside. Maybe he doesn't have keys to the house on him right now. As soon as he leaves, I can lock him out and search for a way to call for help. Then again, he does, at a minimum, have a key for the room downstairs. Maybe the keys are all on one ring together, I've never paid enough attention to notice. If that's the case, locking him out would be a terrible plan.

The sound of his footsteps as he reaches the top of the stairs has my heart in my throat. I'm in the living room, searching desperately for somewhere to hide, when I hear the back door open.

Spying a wooden door up ahead of me, I open it and dart inside.

Darkness greets me, along with several coats and jackets. It's a coat closet, I realize, and I've backed myself into a space with no escape, but I have no time to second-guess my decision.

I'm out of time for everything, in fact. Whatever I did, didn't work.

His footsteps are closer now—so close I have to hold my breath, sure he'll be able to hear me. He's just outside of my door, pacing the living room. Searching for me.

"I know you're still in here." His voice is low and slow. He's in no hurry. I'm a trapped rabbit, and he's the wolf. Waiting me out. "There are only so many places you can hide, Mari. Come out now, and this will be a lot easier." His feet drag slowly along the carpet.

Shhhh.

Shhhh.

Shhhh.

Then faster. *Swish. Swish. Swish. Swish. Swish.*

I'm going to die. Or vomit. Or have a heart attack, then vomit, then die.

At this point, I'm not sure which I prefer.

He's close. His footsteps slow. Long, dark shadows of his feet pass in front of the door, and I hold my breath.

Please keep going. Please keep going.

I slip toward the back of the closet, millimeter by millimeter, not daring to breathe or shuffle too quickly. Then, the shadows are gone. I release a ragged breath.

Thank God.

The door rips open—*no!*—and I'm so thankful I moved. He stares into the darkness, his silhouette outlined by the light glowing in the living room behind him. If he moves things around or turns on a light in here, there's no question he'll see me.

I'm lightheaded, my heart beating against my rib cage like a wild animal demanding escape. It's so loud, he has to hear it. I squeeze my hands into fists, resigning myself to passing out, refusing to release another breath.

Just as my vision begins to blur, he closes the door and walks away. I cover my mouth with both hands, sinking to the ground. I'm so lightheaded I feel like I might still be suffocating, drifting off without realizing it.

I feel like this is all a dream.

What else can I blame for my good and unlikely luck?

Somehow, he didn't see me.

He should've. This shouldn't have worked.

But it did.

Another door opens in the distance, and then he begins to roar.

CHAPTER SIXTEEN

"*Rrrr-aaaaaaaaaa!*"

Something else slams into the wall of the room he's in.

He's thrown yet another thing, launching it across the room in a fit of rage. At this point, it sounds like the house is being torn apart, piece by piece.

"*Where are you?*" he roars again.

I jump as something else slams into the wall. His footsteps are heading in my direction, and I freeze as he passes by my door, waiting. To my relief, his footsteps don't stop. I listen as they echo on the kitchen floor, then the stairs.

Now's my chance. I push open the closet door without hesitation and suck in a gasp. The couch has been overturned, a floor lamp lies on its side, shade askew. His television is face down on the carpet, along with a handful of knickknacks and plants that must've been beside it when he wiped them all off. I eye the front door and ease the closet door shut silently.

I have to go now. It's only a matter of time until he finds me.

Slipping on the boots, I reach for the door but stop in my tracks. A small, white box is attached to the door-frame, a matching piece on the door. I know instantly what it is as I recall the sound I've heard a few times before.

Re-re-re-re-re-re.

An alarm.

It's how he knows I'm still inside. He must've installed a similar one on the storm door, since the main back door didn't have one. If I open this, he'll know I'm leaving. He'll find me. For all I know, the windows all have them, too.

I'm trapped here, and he knows it.

I step back, weighing my options. I could run, try to make it to safety. If I have a plan, I—

Thud. Thud. Thud. Thud.

I hear the sounds of him jogging up the stairs.

He's coming back.

He's in the kitchen already, moving steadily toward me. I have mere seconds before he walks into the room and finds me standing here, helpless and unprepared.

Darting for a room across the hall, I step into an open doorway and search for a hiding place. It's clearly his bedroom. There's an old waterbed in the center of the room and a television that has been ripped from the wall lying on top of it.

I make a quick assessment of the walls in horror. There are so many photos of me here. Pictures from my website and the press, but also images from book signings. There are three different pictures of the two of us together, my arm around him from behind a table where he proudly holds one of my books.

My mind is fuzzy, my stomach tight. My lungs are suddenly in a vise.

Pure panic and outright horror spread through my chest, like roots spreading out and overtaking my body.

I'm going to be sick.

I had no idea whom I was meeting back then. No idea I was standing next to a monster. How could I have missed it? Why didn't I see how dead he is behind his eyes? How did I overlook the pure evil hiding there?

On the wall, there's a shelf with a full collection of my books. None are missing, which means the ones he's been bringing me are extras. He owns multiple copies, just like he told me before. *I probably own more copies than anyone else in the world.* The wall to my right is covered in framed images of comments I've responded to on social media. They're all to him.

Thanks for your support, Chris!

I'm so glad you liked it, Chris!

You're the best, Chris!

Wow, Chris! What a great review! So grateful for your support.

I snap back to reality as I hear him in the living room once more. It sounds like he's searching the closet I hid in earlier again, more thoroughly this time.

With no other choice, I dart into his closet and slide the door shut slowly and silently. It's not much bigger than the one in the living room. I sink down to the floor and pull a stack of boxes around me to shield myself from him, pulling my legs in tight to make myself as small and unnoticeable as possible. The wound on my stomach screams in revolt.

I'm probably going to die today. Soon.

Strangely, I think I'm okay with that. I'm coming to peace with it as the seconds tick on. I tried. I fought. I did all I could do, but there are fates worse than death, and I will not allow him to take me back down to that room to do what he has planned.

I just won't.

Declan would be proud of me, I think. For trying. For fighting back and continuing to try again and again, despite the fear. I need to believe he'd be proud of everything I've done.

I sit in anxious silence, too afraid to move for fear he'll hear me. I listen as he searches another room in the house. I can make out the sound of things being shuffled around, hear his grunting, groaning, and complaining.

"Come out, come out, wherever you are..." he taunts in a low, sing-song voice.

Snapping into action finally, out of my frozen-in-fear stupor, I decide to look for anything I can use as a weapon. There's always something.

My eyes search the dimly lit space. On the top of the box in front of me is a lanyard from an event Chris attended. An event I went to many times. How many times did I meet the monster who may soon end my life?

They say, statistically, the person most likely to harm you isn't a stranger. But he's a stranger to me, even if we've met. I don't remember him, couldn't have picked him out of a lineup. But he knew everything about me.

The truth of that disgusts me. It makes me physically ill to realize I've done this to myself. I'm the one who gave him access to me in a way he'd have all of this information. I'm the one who attended these events. Who chased this dream. Wrote these books. Opened that email. I wish so badly I hadn't.

I wish I could go back to those early days with Declan and just choose another path—one that might not have been riddled with such pain and loss. Every decision has a ripple effect, after all, doesn't it? If I could go back, I would do it all so differently.

Without writing, I would've been miserable, no doubt. But the end result is still me being miserable now. And better miserable with my family than alone, and soon, dead.

I stare at his name on the nameplate attached to the

lanyard, written in scratchy handwriting with permanent marker.

Christian Pierce

Christian, not Christopher, like I'd assumed.

That name scratches something in the back of my brain. It's so familiar, and yet, I can't place it. Is it just from being introduced to him so many times? From interacting at signings and online only? Perhaps. It's a common name, too. I may know it from somewhere else.

But try as I might to justify it or shove the feeling away, something tells me not to let it go. Something tells me it's bigger than that.

Somehow, I think the name means something to me. I just can't put a finger on what that could be.

Carefully, I move things around in the box, sifting through the various items he keeps hidden in here. Mostly, the rest of the box seems to be filled with more memories. More book signing photos of us together, more candid photos of me from the book signings, printed-out email conversations, screenshots from videos I've posted, more framed comments. Apparently, he's only displaying his favorites. Or perhaps he rotates them out. At this point, he could make his whole house a shrine to me and still not have wall space for everything in this closet to be displayed.

"Mari! Jesus Christ! Come out now!" His scream from somewhere else inside the house causes me to jump as I realize how close he's gotten to me. The house is only so

big, and there are only so many places to hide. Slowly, he's figuring out where I'm not, which means soon he'll be able to narrow down where I am.

I put everything back in the box quietly, trying to silence my rapid breathing. *Think. Think. Think. There has to be something else you can do.*

Sometimes my inner thoughts sound exactly like Declan's voice.

When I hear Chris's heavy footsteps heading in the opposite direction, I decide it's now or never. I push the boxes to the side and stand again. He's in the kitchen now. Silverware clatters to the floor, then glasses, plates. With each thing he throws, he growls, curses, or roars.

"I'll find you, you bitch! Do you hear me? I'll find you, and I'll kill you!"

I have no doubts.

There's a single window in this room next to the bed. As quietly as I can move, I cross the room and pull back the room-darkening curtain. We're up high enough on the second story that it scares me, but not so high I think I'll get hurt from the fall. At least, I think my odds are better out there than they would be if I stay here.

After searching for signs of an alarm and failing to find any, I unlatch it from the top and give the wooden frame a hard shove upward.

It gives relatively easily, allowing me access to the screen. It's a small mercy, but I'll take it.

Come on.

Come on.

Come on.

I grab the bottom of the screen by its tiny metal edges and tug up. With some nudging, it comes free, and I push it forward, huffing a breath.

I stare out the window at the ground below, heart racing in my chest. I swallow, clear my head, and force myself to focus on the field in the distance. The tall grass sways in the breeze, so peaceful—for a moment so full of pure panic—I can smell it. If I can just make it there, I'll be free. I can hide in the grass and move freely as long as I stay low to the ground.

I'll figure everything else out when I need to.

Don't think about the fall.

Don't think about the fall.

I swing a leg over the window, and the wood of the frame groans with my weight with a popping *tick-tick-tiiiiick.* My heart plummets. *No.* The sound in the kitchen stops. I lean forward, easing my other leg, head, and shoulders out the window until I'm sitting firmly on the ledge. Without time to second-guess the decision, I launch myself forward, knees slightly bent, bracing for impact.

My feet hit the ground first, and the wind is knocked from my lungs, forcing a loud, painful cough. I roll forward onto my knees, then my shoulders. It's a full somersault like I haven't done since I was a kid, and muscles I'd forgotten about ache in an instant.

But I'm alive. Nothing is broken as far as I can tell.

I push up to my feet, and a pain twinges in my right ankle.

At the sound of his footsteps, I know there's no time

to waste or worry about what might or might not be hurt. If I want to stay alive, I have to keep moving. I take off, thankful for the boots I had the foresight to steal as I jog across the gravel at full speed.

My lungs and legs ache, the wounds in my calf and stomach burning like a stitch in my side, begging me to stop, but I can't. If I stop moving, I die. If I slow down even a little, I die.

I push forward, tears pricking my eyes, and just as I hear the front door's alarm—*re-re-re-re-re*—he shouts, "Mari! There's nowhere to run!"

I reach the field, my whole body collapsing into the tall grass. I check over my shoulder through the weeds to see him looking in the opposite direction, one hand over his brows to shield his eyes from the sun.

With a smile, I let out a silent sigh.

I made it. I did it.

I don't know what will come next. I don't know where I'll go or how I'll make it home. I'm not worried about snakes or any other kind of animal that might be lurking in this tall grass.

I'm just happy. Just free.

I can only focus on my breathing.

Only focus on staying alive.

CHAPTER SEVENTEEN

Once I've caught my breath and my adrenaline has begun to come down, I sit up and check my wounds. My stomach is bleeding again, although not enough that it causes me much worry. My calf is mostly healed at this point, so it's okay, too. There are no other scrapes or bruises I can see, so other than being petrified, I'm doing fine.

All in all, it could be so much worse.

I push myself up to a crouching position and survey the land around me. In the distance, I can see the top half of an old barn above the tall grass of the field.

Chris headed in the opposite direction when he ran past me minutes ago, racing to follow the long driveway. If I can make it to the barn, it might be a good place to hide out with a decent vantage point while I wait until it gets dark. Then I'll be able to make my way up the road in hopes of flagging someone down on the highway.

Hopefully someone less deranged than my current captor.

Deciding that's my best course of action, I push up to my feet. The ornamental grass goes about a foot above my head when I'm standing, but still, I keep bent over, taking advantage of the extra coverage.

I move through the grass slowly, trying to keep my path and movement inconspicuous in case I miss his return. It's easier said than done. The sun beats down on my body, moisture clinging to every inch of my skin from the high humidity. I wipe sweat from underneath my nose, breathing downward through tightened lips to dry my chin. I can already sense that I'm getting sunburned just from being out here this long.

The food I've eaten lately is a shock to my system—lots of processed meals I ate in my twenties but can no longer get away with. Despite losing weight during my time held prisoner, I feel bogged down. Tired. Like I weigh much, much more. I don't remember the last time I ate such little fresh food. Even with the veggies he's brought me, it's not enough to keep me feeling my best. Not that I'm the best person to discuss nutrition, by any means. I prefer potatoes to salads, and wine is my most consumed fruit, but I try. As much as everyone else does. Still, now as I try to move, I have to wonder if there's a reason he's fed me this way.

To keep me weak.

Then again, that could just be the alcohol withdrawal. Even with the two small glasses of wine Chris has delivered to me daily, I desperately want to drink at every moment, even when I have to think about surviving instead. Out here, back in the real world, the cravings are at an all-time high. How sick is that? I'm running for my life and still thinking about when I'll get my next glass of wine.

Now that I think about it, I can't remember the last time I only had two glasses of anything in a day. Usually, I have two glasses before noon.

Maybe I'm getting better somehow. Maybe this actually is helping me in some strange, sick way. Like a forced, psychotic rehab.

That thought makes me move faster. It makes me more determined than ever to keep moving. To prove to myself I can do it. Even when my lungs burn and my stomach aches and my feet sweat... Even when I know I'm going to pass out if I don't stop... Even when my throat feels so thick with cotton I can't swallow... I refuse to stop. I slow down and catch my breath, but I never stop.

When I'm close enough to the barn to see most of it, the engine of his car revs behind me. He's made it back from the driveway empty-handed. I turn around, watching him closely from my hiding spot.

The green car peels out of the parking spot, and next thing I know, he barrels into the field. The car knocks down the tall grass, clearing a path for him as he pushes through.

No.

My heart stops. I turn back to face forward, racing for the barn at full speed. Glancing behind me, it's clear he hasn't seen me. He's just trying to weed me out.

That might be a good pun if I wasn't so terrified.

The car spins circles, zigging and zagging without regard for all he's destroying. He slows down, revs his engine, then flies forward.

Again and again, he repeats the movements, obviously fully prepared to mow me down with the rest of the field.

When I reach the barn, the grass line ends, and I have no choice but to run out in the open. I turn back, waiting for the moment when the car is facing the opposite direction, and then, the second it is, I run as hard and fast as I can. I don't stop until I've reached the back side of the barn, where I rest against it, catching my breath. The car is still driving, but I can't see it from here. I find a small amount of relief in the fact that it sounds no closer to me than it was before.

I release a breath and take a look at the two large double doors to get inside. If they are locked, this could've all been for nothing.

To my relief, as I move closer, I see one of the doors is cracked open and barrel forward toward safety. Inside, the air is shaded and dusty. The sound from outside is slightly muffled, giving me the first sense of peace all day.

The space is dark, so it takes a few seconds for my eyes to adjust before I can make out my surroundings. I search for anything I can use as a weapon but come up empty-handed. The stalls are empty, and there are no tools lying around. I could try to break one of the wooden feeding troughs off of the wall, but I'm not sure I'd be able to and don't want to draw any attention to myself with the noise, so that's my last resort.

Dust flies up under my boots with each step across the dirt floor, and the place smells vaguely of horses, sweet feed, and manure. Memories from summers spent on my grandparents' farm flood my mind. Whatever animals were here, whomever they belonged to at one point, they're obviously long gone.

In the last stall I check, there's a wooden ladder built into the wall, so I cross the barn on my way to it. There's a chance I'll find something of use upstairs.

After testing the wood of the ladder's first few steps to be sure they'll hold my weight, I put my foot on the bottom rung and hoist myself up. I climb slowly and test each additional step before I put my weight on it, relieved when each one holds me without issue.

When I reach the top floor, I walk cautiously toward the far wall and peek between the boards for a look outside. The car has headed in the opposite direction, but he seems to be slowing down.

I hold my breath. If he comes in here, there are a few hiding places, but ultimately, I might've backed myself directly into a trap.

The car turns, and for a brief moment, I'm light-headed. But he points it toward the driveway, and the car jerks forward. Without hesitation, he flies down the driveway, slinging gravel and white dust in every direction. I sink down to the ground with a sigh, then fall backward onto my back.

For the first time, I can catch my breath. While I'm safe—while he's gone—I have to do that. My energy is waning, my ankle has begun to throb, and I fear if I push myself further than I have to, I'll never make it.

I lie still until the sun passes across the sky, casting moving shadows in the room around me. Part of me never wants to move again. I contemplate staying here and dying peacefully, my body turning to ash on the rotting wood beneath me.

It doesn't seem so bad.

Beats the alternative, anyway. But I can't. Some part of me is a fighter—the embodiment of the strong women I've spent the past thirteen years of my life writing about. I can't let that part down.

As the sky begins to darken, I get up and peek out again. The driveway is empty, meaning he still hasn't returned. Wherever he went, it must be far. Then again, I think everything could be pretty far from wherever we are. It feels like we're in the middle of absolutely nowhere.

Maybe he's still searching for me. Or maybe he's worried I've gone to tell someone where to find him, and he won't be back at all.

A girl can dream.

My stomach growls as the evening turns into night. I've wasted enough time now. I need to come up with a plan. Need to get moving again. I wish there was a way to call for help, but the barn isn't equipped with a phone, and there's no chance in hell I'm going back in that house for any reason. I'd rather risk it with the field and highway.

Back on the bottom floor, I check the last room, which is littered with hay, animal feed, and mouse droppings. In the corner, I spot a few random tools that make my heart soar. I rush over and sort through them. There's a rake, a rusty hammer, a broom, and a pitchfork. I pick up the pitchfork, deciding to use it for protection, but also to help me walk, as my ankle is still quite painful when I put pressure on it, and now my wounded leg is beginning to sting. I realize I must've torn open whatever remains of the wound at this point.

Despite how badly I'm hurting, I have no idea where I am or how far of a walk it will be to the nearest highway or town and, as the night progresses, I have to assume it'll only be a matter of time until he returns. As much as I'd like to stay and rest, I need to go now.

I head back for the door and send up a silent prayer.

Sweetheart, if you're up there—if you can hear me— please help me get out of this. I don't know if I believe in heaven, or where I think we go after we die. What I do know is that, right now, I need whatever help and hope I can get.

I step out of the barn and suck in the humid, rapidly cooling night air. Fireflies dance around the field, giving the sky a peaceful glow, filling me with nostalgia for simpler evenings and quieter times. Liam used to catch fireflies in jars when he was a kid every night during the summer. Declan and I would sit on the front porch—or stoop, when we only had an apartment—and watch as he ran around for hours, mesmerized by the bugs. We'd have to wait until he went to sleep to release them, then tell him they escaped and went home on their own while he was sleeping. He believed that until he was ten I think.

Times were so easy back then. What I wouldn't do to go back.

Enough reminiscing, Mari. Snap out of it.

I'm wasting precious time, and I have a decision to make. If I follow this field, there's a chance it goes on for acres and acres with no end in sight. Chris took the driveway and obviously headed somewhere. I think it's my best bet to head in the same direction, though I'll stay in the grass just in case he comes back and our paths intersect.

I barrel back into the tall grass, blades slapping my face and arms as I run. It's scarier at night—all shadows and darkness. Anyone, or anything, could be in here with me, and until I was right up on them, I'd never know.

I try to shake the thought as I hurry along, staying hidden by taking advantage of the tall grass and numerous shadows worrying me so much, using the pitchfork to clear my path and to lean on for support at different times. Mosquitoes have started to bite my exposed skin, and I swat them away, the bites and sweat making me itchy and uncomfortable as I make my way through the field.

When I catch sight of a fence up ahead, my eyes fill with tears.

Please no.

It's a dead end. There's no way I can make it out through here...

The fence completely encircles the property as far as I can see. It's thick and made of barbed wire, each strand no farther than an inch apart. It's much more protection than what's required to keep livestock in, which makes me wonder if it's all to keep me inside or if I'm not the first person he's kept here.

I can't climb over or under the fence unless I want my skin torn to shreds, and since I'm already in rough shape, or unless it's my only option, I want to avoid that. I try pushing on one of the wooden posts, determining whether or not it will be easy enough to push over, but it doesn't budge.

Not that I'd really expected it to.

Resigning myself to the fact that I'm going to have to move closer to the driveway and find the gate that must exist, I hold the pitchfork tighter. I move slower now, keeping my eyes peeled for any sign of movement or the gate.

When I finally find it, I stop in my tracks.

Can this really be happening?

Have I really found the way out?

Am I really going to escape?

I look left, then right, but there's no one there. I'm free. Just a few more steps, and I'll be on my way out of the fence. I reach the metal gate, which he shut behind him, and grab hold of the heavy chain wrapped around the post to hold it in place.

I lift it off and pull open the gate slowly, slipping outside. Instantly, relief washes over me.

I made it.

I did it.

Turning back toward the gate, I wrap the chain in place around where it was before, leaving no trace that I was here.

It takes me several seconds to figure out what happens next.

Lights appear from behind me, flicked on as if by a light switch. I stare in horror at the shadow my silhouette is casting on the silver metal of the gate.

I know who it is before I turn around, and when I do, shielding my face from his headlights with one hand, I spot the green car parked just behind the treeline.

I realize my mistake in an instant.

Stupid, stupid, stupid, Mari.

He knew I couldn't escape the fence.

He knew, wherever I was, I'd have to come out this way.

He just had to wait me out.

I walked right into his trap.

CHAPTER EIGHTEEN

It takes him mere seconds to reach me, and despite the pitchfork in my hand which I wield seconds too late, I can't fight him off. I try and manage to swipe his cheek with the tines of it, but he kicks my shin without missing a beat, and I go down in a second.

From there, he grabs the pitchfork from my hand effortlessly and tosses it away from us, grabbing hold of my arm and jerking me to my feet.

He doesn't say a word as he leads me to the car.

Instead of taking me to the passenger side like I expect, he stops on the driver's side and opens the door. He sits down inside the car, lowering the window, and closes the door without releasing my arm, our hands tucked neatly inside. I'm too scared to ask what's happening or try to fight.

A dull throb in my knee is past the point of being able to ignore it, even through my adrenaline, and I realize when he kicked me earlier, it did something. I can feel it swelling already.

He starts the car, and suddenly, I understand.

"No, Chris, please don't—"

As if egged on by my pleas, he hits the gas. My arm is jerked forward, the rest of my body following suit as I'm forced to run to keep up. He doesn't go so fast it's impossible to stay with him, or that I'm dragging on the ground, but fast enough my lungs and legs burn for relief. Fast enough I know, if I fall, I will be killed in an instant.

The driveway seems longer than ever as he speeds forward, jerking and stopping for periods long enough to give me false hope this torture is ending, but not long enough to allow me to catch my breath. It's obvious he's enjoying tormenting me every painful step of the way.

I think through my options as much as possible while pure panic supersedes all other thoughts. I could try to bite his hand, but our hands are inside the car. If I attempt to, I might trip myself or risk causing him to wreck. Jerking my hand away isn't enough. He's just holding me tighter each time I try.

With each step, a bolt of lightning shoots through my knee. Something is very wrong, and I fear it's going to give out at any second.

Think, Mari.

Think.

I want to give up, to just drop to the ground, to stop trying, but I fear what would happen. I fear I'd end up under the tires, that he'd run me over and still drag me back to the house and somehow nurse me back to health.

That I'd become some Frankenstein-esque monster, pieced together, missing more limbs than I have, scars and fresh wounds covering every inch of my skin, and forever locked in a basement, relying on this man to keep me alive and functioning. Relying on him for everything. Then there'd be no chance of escaping. Ever.

Maybe that's what he wants.

How did this happen? How did we end up here?

Minutes ago, I'd been moments away from freedom. Now, I'm back in his clutches and certain this torture will feel like child's play compared to whatever's coming next.

We don't stop until we reach the house, where he parks, and I double over, panting. My lungs and muscles throb and tremble from exhaustion. Spots fill my vision, and I can feel blood trickling down my side from the wound on my stomach.

I should say I'm sorry. Maybe that would help. But if I speak, if I use my mouth to do anything except breathe, I'm afraid I'll vomit.

He takes hold of my arm and leads me inside without a word, but to my surprise, it's not the lower level of the house I'm taken to. We walk over the devastation of his tirade from earlier, the shattered dishes and scattered silverware. The chairs he knocked over—two of them broken. The food, which he tossed from the pantry, the fridge, and the counters. Everywhere I look, splattered remnants of food clings to the walls, ceiling, and floor. In the living room, there are shattered picture frames and shards of glass littering the carpet, and the couch and lamp are still overturned.

He pushes me forward, not giving me time to take it all in, and before I realize what's happening, we're in the tiny bathroom next to his bedroom.

"What are you doing?" I ask finally, finding my voice.

"Take off your clothes."

When I turn to look at him, his arms are folded across his chest. "*What?*"

"Do it, or I'll do it for you." His eyes flick down to my chest.

"Why?"

In answer, he glances at the shower.

"I need privacy."

He shakes his head. "You lost the right to that. You've lost all your rights, Mari. I'm not going to be so nice anymore. Now, take off your clothes and get in the shower. I won't ask again."

I want to tell him he hasn't asked at all, but I can see in his eyes this isn't the time to press my luck. Turning my back to him, I grab hold of the bottom of my shirt. The fabric clings to my bloody bandage as I pull it over my head. Next, I step out of the sweatpants Chris gave me several days ago, feeling totally exposed. I pull off the bandage on my stomach, wincing as the adhesive is ripped from my sore, sensitive skin. Then I bend and pull the bandage from my leg as well. I toss the bloody gauze onto the floor, wondering vaguely what he'll do with those.

Another thing for the blog I imagine he has?

Something to sell? Something to attempt to clone me? Honestly, nothing feels too far-fetched at the moment.

The cold porcelain of the tub adds to the chills lining my skin as I step inside. I'm still in my bra and underwear, but no matter how much I want to take them off to get fully clean, I refuse. He doesn't seem to be in a mood to argue that minor detail, for which I'm thankful.

I reach forward to turn on the water, but he swats my arm away as if I'm a child not minding their manners. "Sit."

I stare up at him. "What?"

"Sit, Mari. You're taking a bath. My shower doesn't work."

The idea of sitting in the place where his bare body was just hours ago disgusts me. I want to argue, but there's no use.

I sit down in the bathtub, and he turns on the water, making sure the temperature is so hot it scalds my skin. I won't give him the satisfaction of complaining or allowing one ounce of pain to show in my expression.

Instead, I scoop up the water from the faucet and drop it over my face and body. Handful by handful, I use the water to clean myself, to wash away the dirt and grime from the past several days. I have no idea when or if I'll take a bath again, so as much as one can enjoy themselves while being watched by the man holding them hostage, I do.

Eventually, he stands and pulls a washcloth from a closet next to the bathtub, grabbing a bottle of body wash and squirting a glob onto the rough, thinning fabric.

When he hands it to me, I use it to wash my skin,

being extra careful around my stomach wound, my newly sore knee, and my calf. The skin around my knee has begun to purple, but the swelling isn't as bad as I expected. When I look up, I notice he's staring at it, too.

Does he feel bad for what he's done? Does he even care?

Something tells me he doesn't feel much of anything. His face is stoic. Empty. As if he's watching a mindless television show and not the woman he's holding hostage cleaning the wounds he's given her.

The initials carved into my calf will scar, there's no doubt about it. I can't help wondering how many other scars I'll have before he decides he's done with me. Will he follow through with his plan to remove my teeth today? If he does, will I ever eat the same way again?

"What did you do with my things?" I ask, wringing out the washcloth.

"They're gone."

I assumed as much, but the way his eyes flicked toward the wall his bedroom is on has me questioning that theory. Is it possible I was in the same room as my phone earlier? Was it in one of the boxes in the closet I didn't have the chance to search? Is it possible, with just a little more time and a smidge of luck, I could've found it, called for help, and avoided all of this?

"Who is the woman who visits you?"

He narrows his eyes.

"Please, Chris. I just want to know more about you."

His lips pinch together, then break apart with a sigh. "She's no one. Just my sister."

"She sounded worried about you."

He looks away. "It's not like you care."

"Of course I care." I adjust, turning to face him. "Of course I do. I'm just scared. I'm very, very scared here."

"That's good," he says, his voice steady, as if I've told him I'm feeling better after a nasty cold. "The fear is what gives you an edge, Mari. It's why your books are so important. You aren't afraid to write about what scares you, to write about what scares all of us. You used to be brave, but lately, you're hiding in your house. Hiding behind the alcohol. I'm going to teach you how to face those fears again."

I force a soft smile. "You're right. I know you are. It's just hard. You know me so well, Chris."

"I know you better than anyone." His voice is so matter-of-fact it sends bile climbing in my throat.

"I just... I guess I feel badly I know so little about you."

"I'm a nobody." He shrugs me off. "This is the most important thing I've ever done. You are my greatest achievement. Or, at least, you will be."

"It's very noble," I agree. "Helping someone out like you've helped me. I know it comes from a good, selfless place."

He studies me for a long while, and I worry I've oversold it. Then he says, "It was her house. The place I had you meet me. She's a realtor and is selling it. Apparently, the police came around asking about you, asking about that address, and the homeowners started questioning her."

I force down the hope swelling in my chest. "And what did you tell her?"

"I told her I didn't know anything about it. I'd already moved your car. There's no proof I was ever there."

I quirk a brow, the expression causing a twinge of pain from the bruise left by his punch to my face. "Really? A house that big didn't have security cameras?"

"They did, but they weren't being monitored. I hired a realtor to go and check the place out a few weeks ago. I watched her type in the gate code and saw that the only cameras were on the front and back doors. The house alarm code, which I also memorized, deactivated the motion sensors. A week later, I asked to see it again. When people think you have money, the kind of money it would take to buy a place like that, they tend not to ask many questions. I brought some electrical tape with me and stuck a piece to each of the lenses. When I went back a few days later, the tape was still there." He looks proud of himself, and I suppose he should be. As far as plans go, it was a pretty good one.

"So, your sister doesn't suspect anything?"

"It's hard to say." He stands, opening the closet again and pulling out a dry towel. "She doesn't trust me—never has. But she also doesn't understand me. Or try to understand me, for that matter. No one does. No one except you. The you who wrote those books."

"I'm sure that's not true."

"It is." He bends down, pulling up the drain and holding out the towel. "Come on. You have to dry off and go back downstairs. I'm going to be late for work."

"But it's..." In truth, I have no idea what time it is, but it's certainly not morning. "It's not time for school."

He doesn't answer; he just turns his back to me as I gently pat my body dry. He grabs my dirty clothes from the floor, and I wrap my body in the towel, following him out of the bathroom. The promise that he's going to be leaving soon has me filled with relief.

He stops off in his bedroom, digging through his drawers and tossing worried glances my way every few seconds. Finally, he grabs a pair of sweatpants and a T-shirt and holds them out. "Here. Something clean for you to wear."

"Thank you." I take the clothes carefully. I still don't want to wear anything of his. I don't want his scent on me any more than it already is. But as a shiver runs over me, I know I can't be picky. I doubt I'll ever get my clothes back, and I have to wear something. He grabs my arm and leads me through the living room, shaking his head as if he's just now seeing the mess he made.

He takes me downstairs and puts me inside my prison cell. For a second, I worry he's going to demand to watch me change, but he doesn't.

Instead, he looks me up and down, then points to the camera. "I'll be back in a few hours. I have the camera, though, and I'll be watching. Hear me, Mari, when I say this: If you do anything weird, if you try to escape again..." He pauses, huffing a breath through his nose. "I won't hesitate this time. You'll leave me no choice. I'll have to kill you."

CHAPTER NINETEEN

Knowing that I have the house to myself means I can sleep, and despite how scared and worried I am, I take advantage of that. It feels like the first real sleep I've had in so long. Perhaps it's because of how exhausted I am from all of the adrenaline and exertion from the day, but either way, after he shuts the door, and I take off my wet bra and underwear in the corner, away from the camera, I put on his clothes, climb into bed, and the next thing I know, it's morning.

At least, it feels like morning, and I can hear him moving around upstairs. It's noisier than ever before, and I realize he must be cleaning up his mess from yesterday.

It gives me a certain sort of pleasure to picture him sweeping up the shattered glass, righting the fallen lamp and furniture, scrubbing the food from the cracks and crevices of the floor, and straightening the picture frames he knocked down. To know, for once, that he's having to deal with the consequences of his actions is oddly satisfying. And, of course, there's always a chance he could miss something that his sister might notice during her next visit. Something that would lead to her finding me. Something that would be his downfall.

I lie in bed all morning, munching on the grape Life-Savers he seems to have an endless supply of and thinking about what I learned yesterday. The fact that the police showed up at the house means Kassara sent them. It means she's looking for me, that she's not giving up.

The police have to be looking for me, too, still. If they didn't locate me where I was supposed to be, if I didn't show back up at home, they would be trying to search for me somewhere. Does that mean they've contacted the real Owen Doyle? Would they be trying to figure out how someone was able to access his email account? Or spoof it, perhaps?

No one has the password to my email account, but it's possible Kassara could figure it out. Or maybe the police have a way to access it without the password. If they can get into it, maybe they'll be able to trace where the email came from. Or maybe they could see who might've had access to the house where we met, aside from Chris's sister. Is there a chance they'll connect the dots between them? That has to be my greatest hope for rescue.

Unless Chris was lying about that.

He's lied to me about so much else. It's possible he's lying about everything.

I picture a nationwide search for me, picture my name in the headlines for the first time since the shooting. For a reason other than my loss. My deepest pain.

When I first began publishing, I imagined my fame would be instant. I, like all authors—whether or not they'll admit it—thought I was that good. Really, really good. I thought I would be the next big thing. So, when it didn't happen, I was devastated. My career has been fine, don't get me wrong. Modest, but successful enough to write full-time and support myself. Successful enough to splurge for the venti at Starbucks without thinking twice or purchase random things from Amazon without checking my account balance.

Still, my name has never been in the news for something of my own merit. Not then and not now.

Once again, someone else's actions will have determined the story they spin. Will they call me stupid for falling for his tricks? Will they say I deserved what I got? Will they say the police are wasting resources looking for a stupid, fame-obsessed woman who jumped at the chance to change her life without looking into things more? Will tech experts weigh in and say I should've been able to tell the email was fake or hacked or stolen somehow?

Will some of my biggest critics say at least the world will never be subjected to another half-baked Marietta Morgan novel with their two-dimensional characters, juvenile dialogue, and unrealistic plot twists? Or will my death and disappearance be the start of my rise to fame? Like those artists who become popular—more admired, worth more—just after their deaths.

Like van Gogh and Sylvia Plath. People who were never appreciated during their life and will never know the peak of their success or the sheer number of people their work has reached. It's a devastating possibility.

As angry and bitter as those thoughts make me, I can't help feeling joy over the fact that Kassara is trying. Somehow, even in this dim, stuffy room, it makes me feel less alone.

After several hours of cleaning and shuffling around upstairs, the noise stops, and I know he'll be down to see me soon.

I sit up in bed, my latest plan in my head.

Maybe I should just give up. Maybe it would be better if I just accepted my fate and let him win, but I can't do that. I would never let a character do such a thing, and for now, the only plot I can focus on is my own.

When the door opens, I'm waiting on the bed, the blanket pulled up around me. I smile at him, doing my best to look sleepy.

"Good morning."

"Good morning, Mari," he says, shutting and locking the door behind him before heading my way with a tray of food. "Just toast and eggs this morning." His voice is almost glum, like this is a punishment that's hurting him as much as it hurts me. "I need to run to the store later."

"Oh." My face lights up, and it's completely genuine,

because this couldn't have been more perfect if I'd set it up myself. "Is there any way I could ask you to pick something up for me when you go?"

"Anything." He drops to the bed, eyes wide. "What do you need?"

I look away sheepishly, clutching my hands together. "Well, I hate to ask, because you were almost perfect in getting me everything I love, but there is one thing you forgot, and I've been missing it so much."

"What is it?" He glances at the bowl of mostly eaten grape candies.

My lips curve into a small smile when I meet his eyes. "Mint chocolate chip ice cream."

"Mint chocolate chip?" He scrutinizes me. "You've always mentioned Rocky Road in your stories, never mint."

"That was my husband's favorite. But mint chocolate chip is mine." I look down, appearing as if I'm lost in thought. "I don't know that I've ever told anyone that, actually. You might be the only person to know. Except Declan and Liam. And my best friend, Kassara."

He eyes me.

"Anyway, if it's too much trouble—"

"It's not," he says quickly. "I'll get it today."

"Thank you. I was thinking we could have dinner together, if you'd like. And then ice cream." I reach forward and squeeze his hand gently, and he looks down at it, his grin growing wide. "That is, if you like mint chocolate chip, too."

"Yeah, I love it. It's great." I suspect he's lying, but it doesn't matter. He'll eat it if he thinks it'll make me happy.

Looks like you're not the only one who can set a trap, Chris.

CHAPTER TWENTY

I'm not surprised in the least when my door opens several hours later, and he appears with a tray of pizza, my glass of wine—today's says **I'm not slurring my words, I'm speaking in cursive**—and two bowls of mint chocolate chip ice cream.

I smile at him.

It's so funny how we're both acting like nothing at all happened yesterday. How we're being pleasant and cordial as if this is just another day and we're just regular people.

He places the tray on the end of the bed, the glass of wine on my nightstand, and reveals the laptop tucked under his arm. "I thought we could watch another movie."

"That sounds perfect."

"First, I need to check your wounds." He lays the laptop next to the tray on the bed and picks up the first aid kit from the dresser, walking around to me. I lie back so he can examine my stomach.

He presses on the exposed wound gently. "Does it hurt?"

I wince. "Not too bad."

"It's a little warm to the touch. Could be an infection. I'm going to clean it out with peroxide." He dabs a bit of peroxide onto a cotton ball and rubs it over the cut. I suck in a breath through my teeth.

Lowering himself down closer, he blows a soft, slow breath on the wound, easing the pain but probably reinfecting it, too. Next comes the antibiotic cream and a fresh bandage.

"Thank you," I mumble as he lowers my shirt and checks my calf next. "Your knee is swollen." It's as if he doesn't realize he's the reason for that. "Does it hurt?"

"Only when I walk," I say. "It's not too bad."

He grabs the ice pack from the kit and cracks the package to activate it. Then he gently places it on my knee and stands. "Your calf looks much better. It's healing well."

I turn my leg to get a better look at the purple-and-white skin, his initials there now and forever. It takes all I have to smile and nod.

He picks up a plate with a slice of pizza and passes it to me before I reach for the wine and take a drink. "You told me once at a signing that you like supreme pizza, so I had them load it up."

"It looks delicious, Chris. Thank you." I'm not lying. The pizza looks as mouth-watering as it tastes, and I devour the whole slice in record time while he picks out a DVD from the stack. Once he settles on *What Lies Beneath* and pops it into the laptop's DVD drive, turning it on, he begins to eat his pizza, too. By this point, I've already started on my ice cream.

Mint chocolate chip has never been my favorite. In fact, it's probably one of my least favorites, but for this to work, I have to really sell it, and I do.

I scarf down most of my bowl, pretending to watch or care about a movie I usually love. I just need him to leave. I need to come up with a reason for him to walk out of the room for a few seconds.

Just long enough...

"Hey, do you think I could have something stronger than wine today? Like a vodka soda, maybe?"

"I don't keep liquor in the house," he says, his mouth full of pizza. "Besides, I thought you were cutting back." He doesn't bother looking at me as he says it.

"Oh, right." *Damn.* "I just thought since we were celebrating..."

"What are we celebrating?" He quirks a brow.

Thinking quickly, I lift my bowl. "Our second date."

He grins at me, eyes skimming my body. "This is a date?"

Quickly, I clarify, "A *friend* date. Dinner and a movie. My best friend and I have a standing date like this weekly."

His smile dims, and he averts his attention back to the laptop. "Have you seen this movie?"

"Of course. It's one of my favorites."

He nods, finishing off the rest of his slice. "Mine, too."

"What's your favorite part?"

He turns to me. "The bathtub scene, of course. Isn't it everyone's?"

"I guess so," I agree, taking another bite of my ice cream. "Hey, what's your favorite part in my books? I don't think you've ever told me. What's the scene that sticks with you?"

He turns to me, setting his bowl down. "My favorite scene in any of yours?"

I nod slowly. I'm tempting fate here, but I have to try. This could be my only chance. "Yes."

He closes the laptop, silencing Michelle Pfeiffer, and turns his body completely toward mine, thinking. His lips press together. "That's a hard one. I have so many."

"You can name a few, if you'd like."

"No, let me think. I can narrow it down." He taps a finger to his chin ominously, his eyes searching for something that isn't there. Finally, he opens his mouth. "Oh! Duh. I should've been able to answer this easily. It's a scene from *When Night Falls*."

One of my more recent books. I'm surprised. I assumed his favorite scene would be from one of his favorite books. "Really?"

"Oh, yeah. A hundred percent. The part where the boyfriend is the killer the whole time, but you're *sure* it's the best friend. And the boyfriend has taken Nora to a cabin to hide out, so there's all this tension."

I swallow, knowing what he's describing.

"And they're having sex." His brows bounce up. "It's

one of your most descriptive sex scenes ever. And then..."
His eyes flick to my neck. "He bites her and rips the
chunk of her skin out." He puts a hand to his neck,
pretending to tear a portion of his neck, holding his
empty palm up, fingers bent as if holding a chunk of flesh.
"It was so shocking, so descriptive, so gory. You put everything into that one, I could tell."

I chew my bottom lip. "Yeah, that was a lot." I'd been
planning to tell him I wanted to reenact a scene in hopes
he'd leave the room to go get a book, but what if my plan
doesn't work? What if he doesn't leave the room? Or
what if he does, and the plan fails anyway? Is it worth the
risk when the scene he chose is so unbearable? "Thank
you for sharing it with me."

"What's your favorite?"

The question surprises me, but it's given me a chance
to turn this whole thing around. I rack my brain for a
scene I wouldn't mind recreating. "Um... In *Devil Don't
Care*, there's the scene where they're in the car crash, and
Devin has the ice pick with her the whole time, but Ian
doesn't know it. So, when he leans over, she lets him kiss
her and shoves it into his neck."

He smiles. "Your eyes light up when you talk about
your work."

"I miss it," I admit. As the words leave my mouth, I'm
shocked to realize it isn't a lie.

"Do you want to act it out?" he asks, studying me.
"Get a feel for it again?"

I shake my head. "What do you mean?"

"I've gotten to replay some of my favorite scenes to

remind you how much you love this, to bring it all back, but maybe I've been going about this all wrong. Maybe you need to replay some of yours, too."

"Seriously? You'd take me in a car?"

"Obviously not." He purses his lips. "But we could pretend. Obviously, I'm not going to actually let you stab me either."

Like I let you carve your initials into my leg, you mean?

He seems to read my mind because he quickly adds, "I'm not the one who needs refreshing, Mari. I already know how much I love your books. How important they are. For you to feel it—really, really feel it—you have to live the moments as real as they can be. Hurting me won't affect you. It's you that needs to feel the pain. I'm sorry, but it's just the way it has to be." He stands, wiping his palms on the legs of his jeans. "I'll be right back."

I'm still shocked by what's happened, that this somehow worked, and confused about what's about to unfold. But I have no time for that. He'll be back any minute. I lie flat, pulling my knees up to block the view of the camera across the room, and grab his bowl. If he sees that I've done this, I'll just say I wanted to sneak a bite of his since mine is practically gone. I reach across the night-stand and pick up the tube of toothpaste.

I have no idea if this is the best or worst plan of my life as I empty the entire tube into his bowl, the thick, white paste forming a noodle across the lumpy, green melting ice cream. I close the tube and put it back before stirring his ice cream quickly until it's mixed well.

The ice cream in his bowl is a shade or two lighter by the time I'm done with it, but it's hardly noticeable. I put his bowl down, adjust so I'm sitting normally again, and continue eating mine.

Remembering his warning from earlier, I know I might've just sentenced myself to death, but at least I can say I went down fighting.

It's what my characters would do.

It's funny when I think about it. I guess I'm acting out one of my books without realizing it. It's just one I haven't written yet.

CHAPTER TWENTY-ONE

When he returns, my ice cream is completely gone. I place it on the tray next to my plate and lean back against the pillows I have stacked in front of the headboard.

He holds up the book proudly. "Got it."

Now that the excitement of the moment has worn off, the nerves about what's going to unfold next are setting in. I need him to start eating and to buy myself time. "I need to reread it to remember exactly what happens. Maybe I could read it tonight before we do this? Like you said before? And then we can come at it from a fresh perspective."

He flips through the pages. "No need. I usually have them tabbed, but I can probably find it. I'll read it for you."

"Oh. Um, okay. Sure. Thanks." I swallow, preparing myself for the worst. "I mean, how exactly are we going to do this if we aren't in a car and I don't have a weapon? Just fake everything?"

He reaches into his pocket and pulls out a yellow, unsharpened pencil. "Not everything. I thought we could use this as the pick. So you don't actually hurt me, but you get a better feel for the action of it."

"Okay, great." I could shove it in his eye perhaps, but it would have to be a lucky shot, and if I miss, the result would be detrimental. It feels too risky, especially with the door locked and nowhere to run. I imagine him running after me, half of the pencil sticking out of his eye, blood pouring from the socket. It wouldn't be a fast enough method of murder without an escape plan.

He passes the pencil to me, brandishing it like a wand, and continues reading silently, his eyes skimming the pages.

"How about this?" I offer, extending a hand. "I'll find the page while you finish your ice cream. That way, we can keep watching the movie, too, and then, when it's over, we'll do the scene."

He looks up at me quizzically, something worrying in his eyes.

I've pushed too far. Too hard. He knows something's up. He knows I want him to eat his ice cream, and now he won't. Or worse, he'll force me to eat it. This was all for nothing.

He silences my thoughts by handing me the book. "Yeah, sure. Okay."

I puff out a silent breath of relief as he rounds the bed and sits down. It takes every bit of strength I have not to watch as he takes his next bite and opens the laptop again.

I skim the pages of the book, not actually reading anything. Instead, I'm *waiting, waiting, waiting* for him to take another bite. As the movie begins again, he does. A slow, tentative bite, like he thinks I might have placed shards of glass in the bowl in his absence.

After the first bite, he takes a larger one, and I silently revel in my achievement.

I fight against a grin as I read my words, knowing the woman who wrote them would be proud of how far I've come. From not knowing if I wanted to live, from not knowing if what I was doing should even be considered living, to this. To fighting for my life with every fiber of my being.

He shovels another scoop of ice cream into his mouth as Harrison Ford appears on the screen. Declan used to tease me about my crush on him and this movie being the reason it all started, but who could blame me? Even as a murderer, the guy could get it.

With several more spoonfuls of ice cream, he finishes the bowl and sets it down. I watch him out of the corner of my eye, disappointed to see he's not yet dead. I'm not sure what I expected exactly. Maybe an Agatha Christie-esque death: a clutching of his throat, a sudden collapse to the floor, tremors. Something, anything.

Apparently, I'm not as skilled a murderer as my books would lead you to believe. Then again, a lack of internet means I'm relying only on what I know, and though I consider myself a wealth of useless knowledge, my skills, tools, and resources are limited in this room. If I had any number of weapons, chemicals, or poisonous plants here with me, I'd be unstoppable.

He leans back next to me against the headboard, hands behind his head with a smug grin on his face as we watch the movie. Every once in a while, I hear him breathe a bit strangely or see him scratch his neck or move his hand in the general direction of his face, and my chest swells with hope.

Every cough is a sign the end is coming. Every scratch of his nose tells me he's going to fall over at any moment.

But the moment doesn't come. Not for any of the next several minutes. The wait is excruciating.

When I locate the page I've been looking for, I hold a finger on it. I'd dog-ear it if I didn't think he might kill me for it.

I breathe slowly, trying not to think about my family every time I look at the screen. This movie is one of the many things that reminds me of them. So many random, everyday things make me miss them. Chicken parm and burgers with barbecue sauce. *Impractical Jokers*. New shoes. The card game *UNO*. Our kitchen table. Those little glasses that look like cans. And especially these old movies, which I spent so much time watching with Declan and then Liam once he was old enough.

As a kid, he loved the old *Goosebumps* series. I tried to get him to read the books, and though he thought they were interesting, he was utterly fascinated by the show. As a parent, I never would've cared what my child did for a living, what dreams he wanted to pursue. I never wanted to push my goals on him. But I was ruthless in my determination to make him love all things dark and creepy, just like I do.

These days, I wish I'd shown him just a little more light in his short life. A little more love, happiness. I thought I did enough, but once they're gone, we never really know, do we?

All too soon, the movie ends, and we're left in devastating silence. Chris looks over at me, his gaze demanding.

"So... Are you ready?"

I swallow, defeat enshrouding me. Either he has an iron stomach, the poison needs hours to take effect, or they're lying to us all as kids about how poisonous toothpaste is.

I need him to die in this room, to pass out in this room at a minimum, so I have the keys to escape. But it's looking less and less likely that it's going to happen.

Turning to face him, I stifle a fake yawn, hoping I'm not making a grave mistake when I say, "I don't know... Are you sure you want to do this tonight? It's getting late."

He takes the book from my hands, marking the page with his thumb. "It won't take long." I grip the pencil in my palm, running my thumb over the eraser as he opens the book and begins to read.

"The car is moving too fast. I realize it as we round a curve, tires skidding on the gravel road. If he notices, he doesn't care. We take another curve, and this time, the car

slides too far too fast. It happens in slow motion and all at once. We're flying and falling. I put a hand up to stop myself, nearly dropping the ice pick. The car seems to freefall as it skids into a ditch, and a scream erupts from my throat. My stomach lurches as I grab the handle above my head, bracing for impact.

"*Ian reaches for my hand as the car flips. We land on our side with an explosion of glass. I clutch my chest, catching my breath and assessing myself for injuries. I think I'm okay. I look over at Ian, who's looking at me as if he just ran a marathon. His lips curve into a smile. 'You okay?' he asks. I nod as he leans toward me, eyes on my lips. We nearly died, and it's all his fault.*" He drops the book on the bed, reciting the rest from memory. "*As he leans farther across the car, his lips touch mine...*"

He edges forward, and I hold my breath, closing my eyes just before his mouth claims mine. He does it without hesitation, the kiss too aggressive. His teeth bang against my lips, his ice-cold tongue shoving into my mouth with too much force. It takes me several seconds to react—to know, process, and try to accept the fact that he's the first man who's kissed me since Declan. My hand squeezes around the pencil, and I lift it in the air. He cups my skull, tilting my head back so he can continue sucking out my soul. I lower the pencil to his neck, and he jerks back, a hand covering the place as if it were a real wound. I go to roll away, but he grabs me.

His mouth comes back to mine, just like in the book, kissing me through his pain, and I mock-stab him again. This time, he goes off script, shoving his hand up my shirt and launching himself on top of me with a deep, guttural groan. The evidence of his excitement is pressed against my stomach.

I'm going to throw up.

He kisses me again, tasting of garlic from the pizza and too much mint. I struggle underneath him.

"Okay. That's enough, Chris. We're done," I say, trying and failing to push his hand away. He kisses my lips harder, silencing me, and when I hear his zipper, my blood runs cold. "No, Chris. This isn't part of the story. Please. Please stop. You don't want to do this," I whisper, tears filling my eyes.

He freezes suddenly, out of his trance, and jumps back from me as if I'm a flame. His stomach growls loudly, gurgling as he pushes up from the bed. An odd sort of look comes over his face, his skin visibly paling in front of me. Then his eyes widen, and his expression goes sheepish with concern.

"*I need to go to the bathroom,*" he announces abruptly, grabbing his laptop and darting out of the room without another word. He locks the door behind him, and I listen as he rushes up the stairs. I can't help the silent laughter that escapes me.

I wait with bated breath, but it has to be nearly an hour before I hear the toilet flush from upstairs. Then comes the sound of the bathtub faucet. The running water tells me he's taking a bath. That he's made a mess.

I smile to myself. Even if my plan didn't totally work —and maybe it still will—at least it saved me for the night. Better than the alternative.

CHAPTER TWENTY-TWO

Several days pass as I wait to see if Chris will die. At least, I'm fairly certain it's that much time. As always, I have no real way of knowing. Again, the withdrawals begin to hit me, though not as bad this time. I spend a lot of time sleeping, and when I'm awake, I find myself trembling and drenched in sweat, but I manage to keep my food down.

For the most part, from what I've heard, he's spent our time apart in the bathroom, which might be funny if I wasn't down here starving. The grape candies are gone, and my throat is dry at this point, plus my own bathroom bucket has become quite full and the room smells like death, the stench attracting flies which have begun to take over the space. Each time one buzzes past my ears, it's as unbearable as nails on a chalkboard.

If I kill him, will I be stuck in this room forever?

I guess I never thought that part through well enough until it was too late. I expected him to die while he was still down here, so I'd have the keys as a means of escape. I never thought about what might happen if he left the room.

Will I die down here, starving and alone, waiting for someone to find me?

Luckily, my worst fears are soothed when the door finally opens, and Chris appears. His skin is sallow, and he looks as if he hasn't slept in days. He hands me a tray of food, and I grab the glass of water first, surprising us both with that turn of events, and chugging it down. Then, I reach for the wine.

"Sorry. I've been sick." He glances at the bucket. "I'll clean that out when I get back from work. Do you need anything else?"

"No," I say between swallows of wine. When my stomach starts to burn from overindulgence, I place the glass on the end table and stare down at the soup and salad waiting for me. The salad looks slimy, and the lettuce is beginning to brown, but I'm so grateful for food I can't bring myself to care. "Are you feeling better now?"

He nods. "Yeah, it must've been the pizza. You haven't been sick?"

"No, I'm fine."

His lips draw in. "Well, there's lunch. I'll be back this evening to bring you dinner."

"Thank you."

He leaves and shuts the door, and I listen for the click of the lock. When it comes, like always, I dig into my food. The first spoonful of soup burns my tongue. It's warmer than usual today, and a tomato base rather than the broth-based soups he typically brings because he knows they're my favorite. The fact that he didn't have time to let it cool before he brought the soup down, in addition to the hurried feel of his visit, tells me he's running late for work. Staring at the fork he left me for my salad, I realize with a sudden surge of glee he's made a mistake in his rush. In my hand, I'm holding an *actual* metal fork, rather than the usual plastic one. This is the first time he's left me with something sharp.

Could it be that he trusts me now? Or maybe he's testing me? Perhaps, but my theory is that he was just so distracted he wasn't thinking clearly.

I stare down at the fork, running my fingers along the tines. I have no idea how to pick a lock, nor whether or not it's possible to do with this, but since this is his first, and potentially only slip-up, I have to try.

Knowing the camera is still watching me, I slip the fork down to my side and continue to eat my soup, acting as nonchalantly as possible in a moment where I'm trying to determine whether or not I'll be able to escape.

After I've finished my soup, I slip off the bed, fork tucked against my side, and cross the room toward the bathroom bucket just behind the door. It's the one place in the room I'm nearly sure he can't see me on the camera.

Keeping myself firmly against the wall, I sidle up to the door and stare at the lock, assessing it. The chain on the outside is still broken from when Chris escaped—at least, I haven't heard him using it lately nor have I ever heard him fixing it—so theoretically my only obstacle is this piece of metal. If I can figure out a way to pick the lock, I'll be free. This time, with Chris at work, no one will be here to stop me. I lift my hand slowly, staring down at the fork as the idea begins to take root in my mind. Then, applying pressure with my thumb, I push against the three tines at the top. Slowly, they begin to give, each one bending forward. I push until my thumb hurts, the outline of each tine indented into my skin. Then, I turn the fork in my hand and push them back in the opposite direction. I repeat this process over and over, weakening them slowly. As I see the metal beginning to grow thin, my heart picks up speed.

It's actually working.

I push once more, and two of the tines pop off with a sharp *click*. Pulling the third back, it's quick to join them. With the remaining tine, I hold the fork up to the lock and place it inside the bottom. Then I place one of the broken pieces into the top of the keyhole.

I know a little bit about bump keys—the keys used to pick locks—as I've written about them in one of my books. This isn't exactly the same, but if I can manage to get the tine in the right place, at the right angle, I think it might still work.

When I feel the pieces lock into place, I begin to turn them.

Carefully, I maneuver the tines, twisting them gently in the direction they need to go. At first, there's quite a bit of give. The pieces turn easily, and I'm sure I've actually done it.

Then it stops.

Suddenly, both pieces are stuck, and neither will budge an inch farther. Fearing the worst, I pull them out and put them back in, twisting and cajoling them, hoping they'll work. Slowly, just when I'm about to give up, I start to feel a bit of give.

My lungs clench.

Come on.

Come on.

Come on.

Come on.

With a final push, as my fingers burn from the pressure of the metal against my skin, they give some more. The keyhole twists, and I hear the old, familiar *click*.

I release a breath, dropping the fork and broken tine to the ground. Oh my god. *It worked. I did it.*

I twist the handle and step back as the door swings open. I stare around for several minutes, waiting for what, I'm not sure. Maybe for Chris to jump out and say he caught me. To tell me this was a test, and I failed.

When nothing happens and no one jumps out, I walk across the threshold and step out of the room. Even the stale air of the house feels better than the room I've been in. I gulp in the clean scent as if it's water in a desert.

Now I have a decision to make. I could make a run for it, or I could try to search the house for my things. While I desperately want to get out of this house for good, and I know I have enough time for a decent head start, I also know there's the smallest chance he's waiting on the outside of the gate like before. As far as I know, the fence runs around the entire property, so that's my only way out.

Knowing that, I decide I want to search for my things first. If I can find my phone, at least I'll have a way to call the police before I leave the house. They can be on their way to me, so even if the worst happens, I'll have a bit of a reason to hold onto hope.

Though...I have no idea where I am to give them an address so they can reach me. Hopefully the location data on my phone will be enough to do the trick.

I cross the room and climb the stairs slowly, my heart lurching with every sound in the distance. When I reach the upper floor, I check outside. Sure enough, his car is gone.

I release a heavy breath from my chest.

After passing through the kitchen and living room, I head for his bedroom. It's the place I'm certain my things are after our conversation in the bathroom. After the guilty way his eyes had flicked in that direction when I asked about them. I'll only search for a few minutes, regardless. If they aren't here, I'll have to take my chances with the gate. I have no idea when he's going to return, but I still have the vague suspicion he's been lying about being a teacher, especially given the strange hours he's been working lately.

Checking the large clock on the wall, I see it's just after ten thirty in the morning, further confirming my theory. He'd be running very late if he was any teacher I know. Wherever he works, whatever he does, he's lying to me about it.

Stepping inside his bedroom, I cover my nose. I'm quite used to my own bad smells at this point, but his are so much worse. His bedroom reeks of vomit and death. There's a pile of clothes on the floor covered in bodily fluids I'd rather not try to identify.

I decide to check the closet first. The first thing I notice is the uniform for a fast-food restaurant hanging near the back. Something clicks into place for me as I recall smelling fried food on his clothing before. Maybe I was right about him not being a teacher, after all. Without time to deliberate on that, I hurry to dump out the boxes I hid behind before. I rifle through the various photos and memorabilia from my career—more signed copies of my books, photos, framed social media posts and comments, photos of Chris and me at signings. The most disturbing is a clump of hair he's framed, that I can't help wondering how he managed to get ahold of.

No, scratch that. The hair *was* the most disturbing until I find a family photo I'm nearly positive once used to sit on my entryway table.

How could you have possibly found this, Chris?

Still, I don't have time to dwell on any part of the discovery, or the questions it raises. I turn my attention to the nightstand next to his bed, which has a small drawer above a door on its front. I open the drawer first, sifting through a stash of receipts, an alarm clock, and several unmatched socks.

Nothing.

Moving on, I open the door at the bottom. When I do, I can't believe my eyes. There, practically waiting for me, sits my purse. It's as if I've run into an old friend. Seeing something so familiar, so safe—reclaiming what's rightfully mine—brings me the greatest joy.

I grab it, digging through the contents as a sob chokes my breath. *I can't believe I found it. I can't believe I did it.*

Finally, my hand connects with my phone, and I pull it out, staring down at the screen. I press the power button with blurry vision and wait.

And wait.

And wait.

I press the power button again.

No. No. No. No. No.

It's dead, and I don't carry a charger with me. *Shit.*

I search Chris's nightstand with fervor, shoving things out of my way. When I finally locate the charger attached to the wall, I grab the cord, running my hand down to the end to check what sort of charger he has. I'm overwhelmed with relief when I see it matches mine. With shaking hands, I insert the connector into my phone's charging port.

I dance in place, overwhelmed with joy and shock that this is actually working as I wait for the apple to fill the screen. When I stop dancing, I search my purse more. My wallet is still there, lying on top, along with a tube of ChapStick. I pull it out and swipe it over my lips. It's a luxury that once meant nothing to me but now has me feeling brand new. Next, I go through my wallet to make sure everything is still there. Thankfully, it looks untouched.

When my phone screen lights up, I throw the tube back inside my purse and tap the screen.

I want to call Kassara so badly, to hear a familiar voice, to let her know I'm still here, but I have to be smart. *Police first.*

I open the keypad and dial 911.

A woman's voice answers in an instant. "9-1-1, what's your emergency?"

I can hardly answer through my sudden sobs. "Um, I've been kidnapped. I'm being held hostage. I need help."

"What's your name, ma'am?"

"I'm...Mari. Er, Marietta Morgan."

"Okay, Mari." She speaks in a calm, certain voice. "And you said you've been kidnapped? Can you tell me where you are right now? Are you in danger? Is the kidnapper with you at this moment?"

"I'm... No. He's gone. I snuck out and found my phone to call, but I don't know where I am. I'm in a man's house. A man named O—"

CRASH.

I jolt and drop the phone.

"Mari? Are you there?" I can hear her calling me from where the phone rests on the floor, but my only focus is on the sound in the kitchen.

He's back.

CHAPTER TWENTY-THREE

I end the call and try to think as I hear his footsteps moving through the house. I messed up. I really, really messed up. I should've left. Should've run for my life the second I had the chance. I forgot about the camera, forgot that he'd probably be watching it and wondering why I was gone for so long. I'm trapped. I should've stayed on the phone with 911. I consider calling them back, but I don't want him to hear me talking and figure out where I am. There has to be another option. There's a way to send my location via text. I know Liam told me about it before, but I can't remember how to do it. I don't have time to look up the steps.

Deciding on my last resort, I open Kassara's name in my messages and begin to type.

> Chris

The bedroom door flings open, and I'm caught. I press send without looking down, the only thing I can do. Then, I drop my phone to the ground, hands up in surrender, and await my fate.

He crosses the room, eyes wide with horror as he glances toward my phone and then back up at me. "What did you do?"

"Nothing," I say, shaking my head. On the floor, the phone screen lights up with Kassara's name. She's calling me. My heart aches to answer, my fingers twitching with the understanding of how easily I could bend down, pick up, and speak to her again. Maybe for the last time.

There's a pain deep in my chest when I realize I've likely spoken to her for the last time already, and I had no idea when it was happening. I didn't soak it up like I should've, didn't tell her how much I love and appreciate her.

"What did you do?" he demands again, grabbing the phone from the floor. His face is the color of a deep-purple bruise. He ignores the call and swipes down on the screen to press a button. He's turned off my location. Checking my call log, he looks up at me, fury in his eyes. His lips wrinkle together, tight with rage. He bends down and snatches my purse with a growl, then grabs my hand and jerks me forward.

"Where are you taking me?"

"Away."

"Where?" *Not back to the room?*

"We have to leave. *Now.*"

"I didn't tell them anything." Kassara is calling again,

and he presses the button to ignore it once more. "I didn't have time."

"Yeah, well, you've lost your chance for me to trust or believe you. I can't take the risk. Unfortunately for you, I turned off your location, so there's no way anyone's tracking you now. As soon as I figure out exactly what you did, I'll throw your phone out the window on the highway." He jerks me forward and leads me to the back door, then to the driveway, where he presses a button on his key fob and pops open the trunk. He leads me toward it.

"What are you doing?"

"We have to go somewhere they won't find us. Get in."

"I'm not getting in there. I can't ride in the trunk. It's not safe."

His face wrinkles with disgust. "Do you think this is a fucking game, Mari? It's not a game. Get in the fucking trunk!"

I wince at the sharpness of his words and tone. "I... I can't. I get claustrophobic. Let me ride in the front with you." Oh, how I wish I'd thought to bring the fork with me. The simple act of tucking it into my pocket would mean I could shove it into his neck right now and make a run for it.

He scoffs. "Yeah, right. Not a chance. You'd try to flag someone down. I'm not stupid."

I bite my lip, trying to find a way out of this. "I mean it. I can't go in there. I'll have a panic attack. A heart attack. Please. I'm afraid of tight spaces."

"Yeah, well, I'm afraid of liars and going to jail, so tough luck." He grabs the back of my head, shoving me forward so hard my face slams into the rough material of the trunk floor. The fabric scrapes my cheek. I cry out, blood trickling down onto my upper lip from where my teeth hit. He pushes me farther, harder, so the carpet burns the rest of my face.

"Okay." I cry. "*Stop*. I'm getting in." Pulling my legs up one at a time, I climb inside the tiny, dark trunk with a thick lump in my throat. Once I'm in, I roll over, trying to control the fear swelling in my chest. I breathe in through my mouth, out through my nose.

You're okay.

You're okay.

You're totally fine, Mari. Just breathe. Just keep breathing.

He grabs my hand, exposing my palm, and before I can look down to see what's happening, he's closing it over something sharp. Pain shoots through me, white-hot and all consuming. I shriek and gurgle, trying to free my hand, but he squeezes harder, refusing to release me.

I'm dying. Being ripped apart.

My vision blurs from the pain, the edges of my peripheral vision turning gray and fuzzy. I'm going to pass out. I'm going to die.

I'm going to pass out and then die.

When the pain is so excruciating I'm not sure I'll be conscious another second, he releases my hand. I look down, forcing my blurry eyes to find focus as my father's lighter falls down into the trunk next to me. It's one of my favorite things—one of the only things I have left of him. I always keep it with me in my purse.

The thought of Chris touching it renews my fury. I glance at my palm, which is red and raw—already oozing from being seared by the flame. I pull my hand to my chest, tears painting my cheeks. "What was that for?"

"I told you what would happen if you tried to escape again, Mari," he says. My heart breaks as he picks up the lighter and slips it deep into his pocket. He clicks his tongue with disappointment. I want to beg him to give it back, but I know it will be pointless.

"You said you'd kill me." At this point, it's hard not to wish he would.

"I will," he says, shrugging one shoulder. "But I worked hard to get you here. You weren't an easy target, Mari. Do you know how long I've been planning this? Do you have any idea how much preparation it took? I'm not killing you until I have no other choice. We're going to have some fun first."

With that, he tosses my purse in the trunk. I glance over at it, and he shakes his head. "Don't even think about getting any ideas. I've got your phone." He holds it up. "Your friend stopped calling; 9-1-1, too."

I swallow. I didn't realize they'd called back.

"I told you, Mari. I'm the only one who cares about you, the only one who tried to save you, and this is how you treat me. Now you're going to see how that feels."

He slams the trunk shut, and I'm bathed in darkness.

My throat constricts. I can't breathe.

CHAPTER TWENTY-FOUR

I 'm being squeezed to death by an invisible force.

The force doesn't exist. I know this somewhere in my rational mind, but that portion of myself feels long gone. I'm full-on lizard brain at this moment. I can't breathe, can't physically fill my lungs. I'm shaking as if I'm cold, but I'm not. I'm burning up. Sweat drips from every surface of my body, and I'm dizzy and nauseous. I could throw up right now, and if he takes one more curve as fast as the last one, I just might.

My chest is heavy and painful. There's a brick taking residence inside of it.

I'm dying, just like he wanted. I take a small piece of joy knowing it won't be by his hand, that this will be taken away from him, too. Even if I don't manage to save myself, I ruined his plan. One small mercy.

I struggle to take a breath, talking myself down the way Declan used to.

In and out, Mari.

In and out.

I can practically hear his voice.

In through the nose, out through the mouth.

Again.

You're okay.

You're going to be okay.

I follow his instructions, breathing in and out slowly, rhythmically. I place a hand on my chest to feel it rising up and dropping down, my erratic heartbeat just under my fingertips.

I can do this. I will do this. I'm going to be okay.

I squeeze my eyes shut, clutching my hands to my chest. No matter what happens, no matter what comes next, I fought. I tried. Kassara will know. She'll know I fought until the very last moment because I sent that text.

If I die today, it won't be for lack of trying, and that will be my legacy.

Not everything else.

I open my eyes as my heart rate slows down. I search the darkness for anything helpful, moving my hands across the fabric of the trunk around me. It's pitch-black in here. I try to think, remembering anything and everything I've learned from films, books, and my own research.

Suddenly, an idea hits me.

There was a movie about it once...

If I can knock out the taillights and stick my hand out, it might be enough to draw someone's attention without him noticing I've done it. I have no idea if we're still on gravel roads or if we've made it to a highway, nor whether other people are on this road even if we are on a highway, but it's worth a shot. I put my hands up in the air, feeling the rough fabric above my head. In the center, I feel a wire sticking out, but there's not enough for me to grab onto, try as I might.

If this is what was meant to be a tab to pull to open the trunk, he's done something to disable it. He wasn't lying when he said this took a ton of preparation. He really has thought of almost everything. If not for his slipup with the fork this morning, I'd still be in that room.

We hit a bump just as I'm rolling onto my side, causing me to put too much pressure on my stomach wound, and pain ricochets through me. I cry out, momentarily paralyzed by the agony.

Come on. Keep moving. Keep trying.

I put my hands in the general area where one of the taillights should be and press it, feeling for a weak spot of plastic, but I feel only metal. I slide my hand up farther, to places I know it can't be, and back again, sure I'm missing it. Still, there's nothing. No plastic, no light.

When my fingers land on what feels like an edge of carpet, I give it a tug. It comes back with ease, and—*there!* I see the glow of red light around the edges of a panel.

Using my fingers to pry up the plastic edges, I peel it back. My chest swells with pride when I see the light finally. I reach forward, ready to try and knock it out, but my hand is stopped by a metal plate.

I can't reach it. I can't reach the taillight. My hand won't fit in the small opening.

No.

No.

This can't be it. I worked so hard, yet still I'm failing. I can't reach the light, can't knock it out.

They make it seem so easy in the movies.

I refuse to give up. Rolling over to reach for my purse, I dig inside, searching for anything that might give me leverage. A fingernail file that can reach farther than I can, perhaps.

Something.

There's always something.

When my hand connects with something unexpected near the very bottom of my bag, I freeze.

What the...

Kassara.

I pull out the bracelet. I can't see in the dark, but I know that's what it is. I feel along the smooth base, the long straps I once wore every day. I remember her mentioning it, telling me I should bring it just in case, but I'd turned it down. I no longer have the matching one, so it seemed pointless. There's no other explanation for why it's here, though. She had to have dropped it into my bag, as a final safety measure.

My chest swells with newfound hope. She might've just saved my life, but it's a long shot.

My phone is in the car and theoretically should be within range, but there's a good chance he's turned it off by now, or at the very least turned the Bluetooth off, which renders this bracelet utterly useless.

Still, it's something.

I remember when Declan gave it to me, when he had

to go away and take care of his dying mother for a month a few years ago. Though we'd been together—stable and happy—for years and should've, by normal standards, been exhausted with each other, the idea of him being gone for an extended amount of time was hard on me.

When he'd brought the bracelets home, they seemed silly. A child's toy. For teenage couples who were away at different colleges or couldn't stand to be apart for a class. Still, I'd taken it and even learned Morse code like he wanted.

Every single letter.

Oh, how I'd thought it was stupid.

I was angry with him. *We have phones. You can text me. How does this make things any better?*

When we're busy, when we're missing each other, playing phone tag... When you have a million things to do and no time to chat, you can say I love you with a few taps of your finger. Or just one tap to let me know you're thinking of me. And I'll tap back. And he had, right then. His finger touched the screen of his bracelet, and seconds later, my bracelet vibrated, its screen going from black to bright white for the length of time his finger rested on the screen. *To let you know I'm thinking of you, too.*

They turned out to be one of the best gifts he'd ever given me. Even after he returned, the bracelets had remained a fixture in our lives. We'd used them when things were busy at work for him or when I traveled for conferences. I grew so used to feeling the vibrations on my wrist, I still felt them several months after he was gone.

Now, he might just save me after all.

I press the button to turn it on, and the bracelet lights up, filling the small trunk with white light.

Holding my breath, I think over the letters I need to use. I want to give her his name, to tell her where I am, and that I'm in danger. To describe the car. But even one of those would be too many letters, and it will all get garbled.

It hits me all at once. The only real option I have. I already sent her Chris's first name. I just need to give her a last name now. Lifting my finger above the bracelet's screen, I begin to type:

P-I-E-R-C-E

I pause, waiting for a response. When none comes, I tap out his name again.

P-I-E-R-C-E

I press my finger down on the screen, the signal that once had been ours.

Then, I type the name one more time.

P-I-E-R-C-E

I wait in painful silence for the bracelet to light up, to know my message has been sent and received, but there is nothing. Most likely, the other bracelet is still packed away and forgotten about. Most likely, I'm sending these letters to no one.

But if Kassara knows she slipped the bracelet into my purse... I have to believe there's a chance. I have to believe she'd know to find it and turn it on.

I type the name one last time:

P-I-E-R-C-E

Then the car stops.

CHAPTER TWENTY-FIVE

I toss the bracelet back into my purse as quickly as humanly possible and begin returning the panel. As soon as it clicks into place, I shove the carpet back where it goes and try to slow my rapid breathing. Hoping I managed to get everything in order, I lie completely still, listening. I try to determine what's happening. The trunk of the car fills with only the sounds of my breathing as I wait. I'm suddenly claustrophobic again.

He shuts off the car, and the door slams shut. I hold my breath, curling myself into a ball. Are we at a gas station? Could I call for help?

Perhaps he's brought me to the place where he's going to kill me.

Perhaps he's brought me to yet another new home.

As I hear him approaching the trunk, I know I'm too late. Part of me hopes my message went unreceived. If Kassara knows she had a chance to save me and didn't make it in time, I hate to think of the guilt she'll carry.

The trunk opens, and he stares down at me with a look that can only be described as disgust. He hates me, yet he loves me.

He wants to kill me for not writing yet wants me to live well and write forever because he's my number-one fan.

"Where are we?" I ask, sitting up.

"Had to pull over and take a leak." He adjusts himself through his pants in front of me, casting a look over his shoulder. "You doing okay back here?"

He's so odd, the way he truly seems to care sometimes. His eyes search the trunk.

"I've been better."

He grimaces at my dry tone. Then, for the first time, I notice the logo on his shirt. It's not the same as the uniform from the fast-food restaurant I saw hanging in his closet earlier. *What the...*

What are the odds?

"You work for Speak Stream?" My blood suddenly turns to ice. "I thought you said you were a teacher?"

"Used to be," he mumbles, looking away. He goes to shut the trunk, but I refuse to lie back down.

"Why didn't you tell me you work for my audiobook publisher?" I demand.

"Wasn't relevant."

If Kassara got my messages, will she realize she knows him? That she works with him? Will she put it all together?

"How did you hack Owen Doyle's email, Chris?"

He gives a lopsided grin, one corner upturned. "I

didn't. Just had to get it close enough you might not notice it was one letter off."

I swallow. If I'd never opened that email, if I'd trusted my gut in thinking it was too good to be true, I wouldn't be here. That's the cold, hard truth. Curiosity killed the cat, and in the end, it's what will have killed me, too.

"Where are you taking me? What's your plan?"

"We're leaving the state," he says, not bothering to explain more. "We just have to make a pit stop first." He raises a hand again to close the trunk. "Now, lie down. We gotta get moving."

I lie back and allow him to close me into the darkness again. A few moments later, I hear a steady stream of urine hit the ground. My upper lip curls with disgust. Then, he's back in the car, and we're on the move.

If he takes me out of state, my chances of being found are even slimmer. Whatever I'm going to do, it has to be now.

I could try to push forward and break out through the back seat, but then I risk him locking me in. Since I can't find a way to knock out the taillights, I need to get creative.

Luckily for me, that used to be what I did every day. It's what I'm best at.

Thinking quickly, I reach for the carpet and pull it back, prying off the panel again and looking inside. I grab hold of the wires I felt behind the taillight earlier and give them a sharp jerk. They rip free easily, and the light goes out in an instant. Without their wires, I've rendered the light useless, and I can only hope it will mean we'll get pulled over. As soon as we do, I'll bang on the trunk and beg and scream for my freedom. I switch sides, locating and pulling back that fabric as well, then repeating my actions from before.

With both taillights out, it's only a matter of time. Now I just have to wait for a police officer to find us.

I lie back down, closing my eyes and listening to the sounds of the road. I've become accustomed to them in my short time here. A few minutes later, I realize I don't hear the crunching of gravel anymore. We must be on a highway now.

Come on.

Come on.

Come on.

The minutes grow long, the road noise lulling me into a half-awake, half-asleep space. I'm exhausted, my body is sore, and all I want is for all of this to end.

I want to go home.

I want to sleep in my own bed. To eat a meal I've made for myself. To see my best friend. To deal with the trauma of all that's happened.

I want to write.

The thought hits me like a brick wall. All my life, writing has been an escape. It's been the way I've dealt with my feelings, faced my fears, survived my life. The day I lost Declan and Liam, it felt like it was taken away from me.

It felt like, *How can I write, how can I do the thing I love most, when they're gone?*

How is that fair?

I haven't touched a laptop to really try to write since. Haven't allowed the plots in my head to take root. But now, what I want more than anything else, is to tell my story.

The brutal, terrible truth of it all. The day I lost them, the day my life fell apart, all the painful moments I've had to live with since then. And this, which in all reality, could never compare to that.

Not for me and not for everyone else involved.

When I feel the car slowing down, my thoughts halt. From the front of the car, Chris curses loudly, then even louder.

Is it working? Did it—

"No!"

CRASH.

The moment is incomprehensible. The pain hits me before I register it. I'm thrown forward into the back of the seats, and suddenly the space is smaller. I'm pinned in between sharp metal and the hard, unyielding fabric on the back seat. Stuck.

I can't breathe.

Can't think.

I've been torn apart.

Warm liquid surrounds me, though whether it's blood or urine, I can't be sure. Half of my body seems to be missing.

I'm dying, or perhaps already dead.

My thoughts come in fragmented pieces.

What happened?

How is it possible to hurt so badly and feel nothing at

all? I'm numb, and yet my body is on fire. Whole, yet scattered. My head throbs. My arm is somewhere underneath me, bent at an angle that isn't natural. I can't feel my legs. My stomach feels ready to combust.

Ow.

Somewhere in the distance...perhaps in another world—in another galaxy or universe yet to be explored—a door slams.

"What the fuck?" *Chris.*

"Your taillights are out, bro. I'm sorry. I didn't see you were stopping until it was too late. *Shit...* Are you okay?" *Someone else.* A voice I don't recognize.

No, I want to scream. *I'm not okay. I'm in here. I'm trapped.*

Help me.

Save me.

"My taillights?" Chris again, sounding angry and confused.

I'm fading. Nothing makes sense. They're still talking, but I can't find the focus to hear them. My world is being muffled with white noise. I'm sinking.

Sinking.

Sinking.

The pain that once existed is gone. I feel lighter than air.

As if I'm gone, but not.

Here, but not.

"Listen, we don't need to get the insurance involved. If we do, it'll be your fault. You're just a kid. I remember when I was your age." Chris. "Seriously, your truck isn't so bad, and I can afford to have mine fixed. I don't want this to affect your insurance or for you to go to jail or anything. No harm done."

"Are you sure? Your car is... I mean, I shouldn't... We should call the police. Or my mom."

"I'm positive. I'll get it taken care of."

Save me.

Save me.

Save me.

A car door slams. Chris curses again. He roars.

I open my mouth to cry out, to beg the boy to stay. He's just a boy. Probably around Liam's age. Seventeen. The age he'll be forever. If I tried to draw his attention, he could end up dead, too. I can't do that, but luckily, before I can utter a word or make a decision, darkness and peace like I've never known take me under, and I'm gone.

CHAPTER TWENTY-SIX

Save me.

It's the first conscious thought I have when I wake.

The second is: *Ow. Ow. Ow. Ow. Ow.*

The pain radiates through me in waves—terrible one minute, worse the next. I squeeze my eyes closed, trying to make sense of the darkness. Of the pain.

I don't know what happened or how I got here. Or where *here* is.

My eyes burn. My skin burns. Everything burns.

I feel like I've been set on fire.

I wiggle my fingers, relieved to find they're all in order, though they feel stiff and sort of...off. I try for my toes next, but it's as if they don't exist. I don't know if I'm making any sense. I don't know why I'm not dead.

It feels very much like I should be dead.

The car isn't moving.

I don't know whether that realization should make me relieved or worried, but it successfully manages both.

At least we aren't still driving. At least there will be no more accidents.

Has he already gotten me out of state?

Surely not. I can't imagine he could drive the car very far in this condition. Especially because it would risk getting pulled over. Perhaps we did get pulled over, and I was passed out through my opportunity for escape.

How long have I been unconscious?

What if he abandoned me? What if I'm going to die here, trapped?

That's when I hear his voice.

"Stay in the car. I'm going to the door."

"No way." That's Kassara. "I'm coming with you."

Tears fill my eyes. It's a hallucination. It has to be.

I fight with all my strength to move my hand, but I can't. I release a sound that feels more like a gurgle than a scream. *Please.*

"Did you hear that?" It's him again. I'm sure of it. Then again, my head is currently stuck to the back of the seat in my own blood, so how can I be sure of anything?

"What?"

"A sound. It sounded like someone crying."

I do it again, pushing noise from my throat with force. *"Aghhh..."*

"I heard it," Kassara confirms.

"It's coming from the car."

Then, they're close. They're so close I can practically smell his cologne.

"*Aghhh...*" I cry again, the sound ripping from my chest. It hurts. It all just hurts.

"Is it possible?" Kassara asks. "Dec, if she's in there... There's no way."

I want to bang on the roof, to scream and cry tears of joy, to warn them, to say, "I'm here! I'm right here!" But I can't. I feel myself slipping out of consciousness again, and it's all I can do to fight it.

"This is his car," he says firmly. "Check the plate."

"What do we do?"

"Excuse me, what the hell do you think you're doing?" Chris has joined the conversation.

"*Chris?*"

"Kassara? What on earth are you doing here?" His voice is calmer. Perfectly polite. Like he's seeing an old friend.

"I need you to open your trunk," Declan tells him firmly, interrupting the reunion.

Yes. Yes. Open the trunk. Find me. Save me.

"Well, as you can see, I was rear-ended in a parking lot today. The person responsible didn't even have the decency to stop and leave their information. With the damage, opening my trunk is impossible." If I didn't know better, I'd swear he was innocent. He sounds so incapable of harm. "Do you mind telling me what seems to be the problem, Officer?"

"Open your back door, then. I need access to your trunk."

Chris's tone turns cold. "Do you have a warrant?

Kassara, what's going on? What are you doing at my sister's house in the middle of the night?"

"Just do what he says, Chris. Please."

"Fine," he says. "I just need to get my keys."

"That's okay." I hear a sudden shattering of glass, and then the back door is open. I can practically feel him through the wall of the seat that separates us. He's just inches away from me. Inches away from finding me. Saving me. I try for another sound, but I'm too tired. I can't do anything but lie here with my hope.

"Mari?" he calls. "Mari, can you hear me?" I feel him bump the seat, feel the vibration of it.

"*What the hell?* You can't just do that! You can't just break someone's window!" From somewhere in the distance, Chris is shouting, "I'm going to call the police. I'm going to tell them—"

"I am the police, motherfucker," Declan says. "And trust me, the others are on their way. Now stand over there and shut the fuck up."

"Mari? Can you hear us?" That's Kassara. Her voice is soft and soothing. I swear it seems to ease my pain.

"Chris? What the hell is going on?" The woman's voice from before, Chris's sister, is here now.

"Go back inside," he warns.

"Why are the police here?"

I feel someone moving the seat again, the hard wall I'm lying against shifting. Then, it collapses, and in mere seconds, I'm free. My body falls forward, no longer pinned in place, and I stare up at the two faces I thought

I'd never see again. Their faces are beautiful and perfect and real and here.

They're here.

This isn't a dream. It can't be a dream.

"Oh my god." Kassara's horror-stricken expression tells me all I need to know about my current state and how bad it is. "Declan..." She looks at him, not me.

I open my mouth, trying to form words, but there are none.

"She's okay," he says, but even I know he's lying. "She's going to be okay. Can you hear me, Mari?"

I try to nod, but I'm not sure it works. I blink instead, tears filling my eyes.

His hard expression softens as he smooths a hand over my cheek. "I'm so sorry. I'm so sorry I wasn't here. I'm so sorry we couldn't find you."

It's okay, I tell him silently. He seems to understand. We've always been able to do that. He dusts a tear from my cheek, but when he pulls his hand back, I realize it's blood instead. "Stay with her," he tells Kassara. "Keep her conscious."

She nods as if she's accepting a mission.

Then he's back out of the car, gun drawn, pointing it directly at Chris.

The sight of him holding it, the sight of him ready to fire his weapon, takes me back. Takes me under.

Bile rises in my throat as I begin to fade out.

"Mari? Mari, stay with me, okay? Please stay awake." Kassara pats my cheek frantically, but it's no use. I want to stay, but I can't.

I welcome the darkness this time as it swallows me, knowing anything is better than this. Even death.

WHEN I RECEIVED *the call that there was an active shooter in my son's high school, I'd been in the middle of folding a load of laundry. It was just another Tuesday. Another day of the beautiful monotony that was my life, and in a split second, it shattered into a million pieces.*

I didn't remember getting into the car or most of the drive to the school. I tried to call Declan a thousand times. Honestly, it was a miracle I made it there without having an accident.

When I couldn't reach him, I called the station, and the kind receptionist—whom I'd met countless times at Christmas parties and when I'd visited him at work—patched me through to the chief. I knew then it wasn't good. Whatever news I'd be receiving, it wasn't good.

"We haven't heard from him, Mari. Last contact we had, he had the shooter trapped in a classroom. He was waiting on backup. Backup arrived, and they were both gone."

The words washed over me, every bit as real as they were impossible.

"And Liam? Have you heard if he's safe?"

"That would be a question for the school, but on a personal level, no. I'm on my way there, but I haven't heard from anyone who's seen him. It doesn't mean anything, Mari. We'll find them."

I knew he was lying. I understood why.

When I pulled into the designated pick-up area, it was barricaded to keep people back. I could see the school in the distance, but they weren't letting anyone through. The street was filled with ambulances and police cars; children hugging their friends and classmates with tears in their eyes; parents aimlessly searching for their own children.

I pictured Liam's dark curls, tan skin, and beautiful brown eyes. I knew he had to be somewhere looking for me, that he must be so scared. When I saw an officer with a clipboard I vaguely recognized from Declan's department, I approached him.

"I'm... I'm looking for my son."

"Name?" He hardly looked up from his clipboard.

"Um, Liam Morgan." It sounded more like a question coming from my mouth. A question whose answer terrified me. "My husband, Declan, is an officer in the building. If you have any updates on him..."

The man's eyes widened as he looked up at me, cutting me off. "You're Declan Morgan's wife?"

I nodded. "Is he okay?" I squeezed my trembling hands together. *I can't lose him. I can't.*

"Ma'am, I need you to come with me." He gestured for me to follow him, leading me away from the crowd and toward two other officers I vaguely recognized. "Is the captain here yet?"

The captain... My blood ran cold.

The officers shook their heads.

"This is Mari Morgan, Liam's mother," he introduced us. "Declan's wife."

Their expressions instantly went solemn, and I knew he was gone even before they'd said it. "Ma'am..." The first officer lowered her head. "We received word just a few moments ago that your husband took down the shooter."

My heart fluttered. "He... He did? So, he's okay? He's alive? Can I see him?"

"Not yet," she said cautiously, and I sensed there was more.

"And Liam? Is he okay?" I knew the answer before she said it. I could see it in their eyes. I just wasn't prepared for what came next.

"Your son, Liam... Ma'am, I'm so sorry..."

Sobs tore through my chest as I reached hysteria. He's gone. He's gone. "He's gone, isn't he? Please tell me he's not gone."

"Ma'am... Liam was the one shooting."

I'M JOLTED back from my memories, more painful than any reality, and Declan is still holding the gun pointed toward Chris, who looks positively furious.

Kassara holds my face in her hands, staring down at me. "She's back," she announces to Declan, as if it's a good thing. She brushes away tears and blood from my face. "Stay with me, okay? The ambulance is on the way. Just hang on. It's going to be okay."

It's not, I want to tell her. It's never going to be okay. How could it?

After Liam's death, Declan left me. He couldn't take

the guilt of what he'd done when faced with an impossible decision. Couldn't look me in the eye when he knew he'd done his duty, made the hardest decision of his life when a killer wouldn't stand down, and in the process, took our only son away from me.

In truth, I couldn't stand to look at him either. How could he do it? Duty or not, he was his father. He'd brought him home from the hospital, taught him to ride a bike, taken him fishing, taught him to drive. He'd loved him as much as I had—with his whole heart.

Then, he looked him in the eye and took his life.

I knew he didn't have a choice. Declan would hardly talk about it, but I'd gotten the story from other people. There was no choice. If he hadn't killed Liam, other innocent people would've died.

On paper, those were the facts.

It was his job. I understood his sense of duty and the fact that he was saving lives, but Liam was our son... If I was in his shoes, I'm not sure I would've made the right call. And I'm not sure I can love him knowing he did.

We'll never understand Liam's actions that day, but we have had to live with the consequences. His choices ripped our city apart. Ripped our family apart. They devastated me in a way I never knew possible. He took two lives. Stole two lives. And no matter how much I love my son, his memory will always be tainted by the atrocity he committed that day.

We thought we'd done things right. We taught him about guns because of Declan's work. We taught him how to be safe. That guns weren't toys. But in the end, we didn't do enough.

Didn't teach him enough.

Didn't love him enough.

And that destroyed everything.

I watch my husband now, the man I haven't seen in over a year, as he points a gun at the man who tried to kill me. He's been on desk duty since the shooting, with no end in sight. He could go back if he wanted to, but I know he doesn't. I don't think he'll ever go back out on the streets.

Perhaps after tonight, none of us will do anything.

Kassara holds me, brushing hair from my face, a phone pressed to her ear. I don't recall seeing her pick it up. "The police are on their way. Just hold on, Mari. Please, just hold on. They're so close."

"How..." I croak. *How did you find me?* is what I want to ask.

"The bracelet," she whispers, her hand gently stroking my arm. "I made Declan find his and turn it on the second you didn't come home. We've had the police searching for you... I'm so sorry. We did everything we could, but it wasn't enough."

"Don't move," Declan commands. When I look up, I watch as Chris takes a cautious step toward the house. I see the pain on my husband's face and know he's reliving his worst moment. This is probably the first time he's held a gun since. I can see how deep inside his head he is. He wouldn't do this for anyone but me. The pain, the utter heartbreak on his face, devastates me.

His hands tremble just enough for me to register it. "Don't make me do this." To Chris, and perhaps to everyone else, he seems sure of himself, but I know him better than I know myself. I can see the pure terror in his eyes.

I hate Chris more than ever for this moment. Of everything he's done, forcing Declan to go through this feels the most unforgivable. The most heinous.

"What is happening?" Chris's sister begs through her sobs. "Can someone please talk to me? Who is that woman, Chris? Why was she in your trunk? What is going on?"

"Go back inside, Jenn," Chris commands.

"If she moves, I'll shoot her," Declan shouts, lifting the gun to point it at Jenn. "Your brother kidnapped my wife. He took her and held her hostage. And, by the looks of it, he had an accident with her in the trunk and left her to die."

"No. He wouldn't. You wouldn't, right? Tell him, Chris. Tell him it's not true," she begs.

"I thought she was already dead," Chris says. "I thought... I mean, I-I thought th-there was no way she could've survived... You have to understand, I never meant to hurt her. I was trying to help her. Jenn, come on. You know I wouldn't hurt anyone."

I squeeze my eyes shut, reliving the horror in that lie. Kassara rubs my cheek, dusting away a tear I didn't know had fallen.

"The police are at your house now," Declan says. "Gathering evidence to prove otherwise."

"And why are you here?" Jenn asks. "If the police are there?"

"Because I couldn't leave it to chance. They went to Chris's house, but I found out you were his closest relative. After the 9-1-1 call we received and the message with his name, I knew he'd be on the run. I disobeyed orders, refused to wait for the other officers to find her. I couldn't lose her." His voice cracks, and I hear the word he's not saying. "I couldn't lose her, *too.*"

It was a gut instinct, and he'd made the right one.

Any longer, and I might not have made it.

"I also..." Declan starts, his voice catching. "I also found out you used to work at our son's school."

Kassara rubs her hands over my face again, and I get the feeling she's trying to cover my ears. "The ambulance will be here soon. Just hold on."

"You were there when the shooting happened," Declan says.

"When he killed two of my students, you mean," Chris says, venom dripping from his words.

"You were fired for leaving the door open."

Somewhere deep in my chest, I feel a tightening sensation.

"I was given the option to resign, yes. So?"

"And then you took a job with my wife's best friend."

"It was a coincidence."

"Everything's a coincidence, isn't it?" Declan sneers. "You didn't start at the school until a year before the shooting. You were the one who convinced Liam to join the drama club, which you led."

"He was a bright boy."

My stomach clenches harder. Suddenly, I'm dizzy. *What is Dec implying?*

"You convinced him to do it, didn't you? You helped him get the gun. We could never figure out where he got it... He was a good boy. Until you got to him."

"Your son made his own choices that day," Chris says softly. Then, for the final cut, he adds, "Just like you did."

I know, without him saying the words, that he did it. That he somehow caused everything that happened. That he's worked his way into every aspect of my life. That's why he had the family photo from our house. That's why he's done all of this.

For me.

Losing Liam.

Losing Declan.

The two other children who died that day.

It's all been because of me.

"Why?" Kassara asks, crying beside me.

"I love Mari like no one else can," he says, turning his head toward me with an affectionate smile. "Like none of you can. I'm her biggest fan."

"You don't know her. You know her books. You don't know who she is," Declan argues.

"Oh, I think you'll find we know each other quite well at this point..." He cackles, and my body begins to tremble.

The trembling doesn't stop, and suddenly, I'm shaking harder. *Something's wrong*, I want to tell them, but I can't. I can't say anything. My jaw is clenched, unmoving. I stare at Kassara in horror, hoping she'll understand.

"Declan! Something's wrong." Kassara's voice is garbled beside me, slow and underwater. My vision blurs as I feel Declan's hands on me.

When I open my eyes, Chris has disappeared, but no one seems to have noticed. I want to warn them, but I can't.

"Baby? Mari? Mari? Can you hear me? Mari? *Jesus, where is the ambulance?*"

CRACK.

A gunshot rings out, and Declan jumps away from me. "Fuck!"

"*Chris, no!*" Jenn screams.

CRACK.

Another.

Chris is back. He's holding a long shotgun and shooting at Declan, who narrowly misses the bullet.

He's going to kill us all.

CRACK.

This time, the sound comes from Declan's gun. I watch as he drops it to his side, his face wrinkled and unreadable. I no longer see Chris. He's fallen behind the open car door.

There are no more gunshots, but the night is filled with so much other noise.

Jenn is screaming and crying, shouting Chris's name. Kassara's holding me tighter, whispering in my ear that it's all going to be okay. She's refusing to look toward Declan, and I suspect I know why.

I can't stop shaking; the movements are so rapid and abrupt it hurts. Then, I see the lights. They're here, but perhaps it's too late.

The rest comes to me in flashes.

Declan doesn't release my hand as they load me onto the stretcher. There's an apology in his eyes and so much left unsaid, but I feel it all. On the ground, Chris lies in a puddle of blood next to his shotgun.

He fired the first shot.

It's all I can think of as I finally fade out, no longer fighting. He fired the first shot. He tried to kill me. To kill us all.

He's the reason my son is dead.

He's the reason for so much pain and misery.

Declan killed him, and I'm glad he's gone, but I wish it could've been me to take him out for good.

"You don't," Declan says, and I hadn't realized I'd voiced that thought out loud. Tears well in my eyes as I see everything unsaid in his expression. He's glad he took the choice, the pain, from me. He's glad I don't have to live with this decision, or the other one. He'd gladly take away my pain and guilt to bear the brunt of that for me.

When he leans down over me on the stretcher, I turn my head slightly, resting against his chest and shaking with sobs. We don't let go of each other until we reach the hospital, Kassara right by my side.

I'm going home.

I'm safe.

I'm going to be okay.

I fought like hell, and just like the heroes I write

about, I never gave up. Looking at Declan and Kassara, knowing I still have them, that I've always had them, I'm so thankful I didn't.

Chris took so much from me, but I'm grateful for what—and whom—I have left.

CHAPTER TWENTY-SEVEN

ONE YEAR LATER

They call me a survivor in my support group, but I don't always feel like a survivor. Sometimes, I just feel like a fraud.

I was lucky.

Yes, I fought, but in hindsight, I failed. If Declan and Kassara hadn't gotten my messages, I likely would've died in the trunk. The actions that I took—pulling the wires to disable the taillights which resulted in the crash, yes, but also publishing my books in the first place and then going to the meeting with Chris, are what led me here.

We've learned a lot about Chris in the past year, most of which I never wanted to learn and would just as soon not know. After a thorough investigation, the police now know he became a teacher at Liam's school after he discovered it was where he attended. We finally understand that he befriended Liam with the intention of getting him out of my life. It breaks my heart to know my son trusted him, looked up to him, and he was betrayed and used in such a way.

We understand based on emails and chats they found on Chris's computer, conversations he had with Liam—that he made him feel seen and protected when he was experiencing bullying. I'll always regret and never understand why Liam was never fully open with us about that. We know whatever role Chris played in helping Liam make his decisions about that day, he was the one who acquired the gun for him.

In journal entries found by the police, Chris claims he did it so he could clear away the "noise" around me. He wanted me alone and was willing to take down everyone surrounding me to make that happen. Getting Declan out of the picture, too, with that one simple act, was just icing on the cake. He would've gotten him another way if it hadn't worked out like that.

He never said as much, but I now understand he would've stopped at nothing to get me in that room. In the house his grandparents left for him after their deaths. The house he'd spent years preparing for my capture. The house I was meant to live and die in.

We also know that, after he was investigated and ultimately deemed innocent for leaving the door open, he was forced to resign from the school. Because of that, he began working at a local fast-food restaurant, which was why I found the uniform in his closet and why he so often smelled of burgers when he was with me.

I don't know this for certain, but I assume the reason he began working with Kassara at Speak Stream as his second job was to get her out of the way, too. I'm forever grateful he didn't see that plan through.

Some days are harder than others. I wish I could say this experience healed me, made me realize how special and precious life is, and that I'm traveling the world and telling my story to help heal the masses now, but it would be a lie.

More fictional than any of my novels.

Most days, it's hard to get out of bed. But I do. Declan comes over to visit now. We're speaking again. Trying again. Things aren't fixed between us—they never will be. Not because I don't forgive him, but because the pain between us is a deeper rift than could ever be mended. There's too much pain and loss in the space that separates us.

When he isn't here, Kassara is. She makes sure I eat, that I continue to stay away from the alcohol—maybe the one good thing that came out of this whole ordeal—brings me my laptop when I feel like writing, and helps me into my wheelchair when I feel like leaving the house.

Not that that's often.

I guess, in a way, I've been punishing myself over the years for what Liam did. That's the one thing I've learned in my group. That because my son's last choice was a horrible, incomprehensible one, I've stayed in this town, in this house, isolating myself from everyone in order to absolve him of his punishment.

But I didn't make Liam's choices.

I'll never understand why he did, and I'll both hate and love him every day for the rest of my life because of it. That's my burden—loving someone capable of monstrous things.

Still, I'm trying to move past it. Not move on, because that's impossible. Just move forward. I'm trying to write again, and if you're reading this, it means I have. It means I was finally brave enough to face the fear and tell my story.

It's not easy—life isn't easy. And I certainly don't ask for your sympathy or kindness. I just wanted the story they tell about my life to be mine.

Not the media's, and certainly not Chris's. I've heard they're making a documentary about his life and death. Watch it if you want to, but I'm sure they'll butcher it.

Whether or not the media accepts it, only two people truly know what went on in that room—him and me.

And, well... I guess if I ever work up the nerve to publish this... If you're reading this somehow, now you know the truth, too.

WOULD YOU RECOMMEND DO NOT OPEN?

If you enjoyed this story, please consider leaving me a quick review. It doesn't have to be long—just a few words will do. Who knows? Your review might be the thing that encourages a future reader to take a chance on my work!

To leave a review, please visit:
kierstenmodglinauthor.com/donotopen

Let everyone know how much you loved
Do Not Open on Goodreads:
bit.ly/donotopenkm

STAY UP TO DATE ON EVERYTHING KMOD!

Thank you so much for reading this story. I'd love to invite you to sign up for my mailing list and text alerts so we can be sure you don't miss my next release.

Sign up for my mailing list here:
kierstenmodglinauthor.com/nlsignup

Sign up for my text alerts here:
kierstenmodglinauthor.com/textalerts

ACKNOWLEDGMENTS

As an author of thrillers like Mari, I tend to write about the darkest and most disturbing parts of humanity. I do this for a few reasons. Number one is that I love puzzles and mysteries. Growing up on *Scooby-Doo, Goosebumps, Are You Afraid of the Dark?*, and *Nancy Drew*, I've always been fascinated by all things dark and creepy (again, just like Mari. I always put pieces of myself into my characters, but Mari has maybe the most of any character so far). Another reason I enjoy writing thrillers is that, in nearly every story, there is someone trying to do the right thing. To save the day. To protect the ones they love.

To appreciate the light, we have to be willing to look into the dark. To show how good people can be, I have to show you the evil, too. I love telling stories where good trumps evil, where justice is served, and where the person who deserves a happy ending finally gets it. The last reason I write thrillers is to explore fears of my own. Most often, my story ideas stem from things that scare me, worry me, and keep me up at night. Writing these stories is a way for me to process the fears, insecurities, and stressors that I have in a safe way. Writing this story was a grueling process for me because it dealt with many of my worst fears and worries. Because of that, this has been probably my most vulnerable writing experience as an author, but also as a woman and mother. I appreciate you taking a chance on this book and going on this journey with Mari and me. It means the world.

Without the following people, I would've never been brave enough to write anything so close to the bone.

To the world's best husband and sweetest little girl—thank you for being here for me through every part of this beautiful and terrifying career. Thank you for cheering me on, believing in me, celebrating with me, and always being in my corner. I'm so grateful to be able to do this with you both my side. I love you more than you'll ever know.

To my incredible editor, Sarah West—thank you for always going with me no matter where I take us with each story. Thank you for believing in and championing each one with unending enthusiasm. I'm so grateful for your advice, insights, and support.

To the awesome proofreading team at My Brother's Editor—thank you for being the final set of eyes on my stories and making sure they shine!

To my loyal readers (AKA the #KMod Squad)—I never know what to say here because nothing could ever be enough. Thank you for trusting me to take you on a whirlwind journey again and again. Thank you for loving my characters and stories as much as I do. Thank you for being excited for each new novel, no matter how different it is from the last. Your support, your belief in me, and your appreciation for my art is something I never imagined I could earn in my wildest dreams. Years ago, when this was all just a dream, I wished for you. I had no idea just how beautiful, amazing, and life-changing you would be. Thank you for coming along for the ride every time.

To my book club/gang/besties—Sara, both Erins, June, Heather, and Dee—I'm so grateful for you all. Thank you for loving my stories, but also for loving me. For welcoming me into your group two years ago and letting me stick around. Every day, I'm so glad you found my books and that they brought us together. I don't know what I'd do without your friendship, without the many tears and many more laughs, without the inside jokes, and without our weekly venting sessions. I can't tell you how much you all mean to me. Love you, okay? Cool.

To my bestie, Emerald O'Brien—my friend. My Maya. My Michael Scott. My moon-sharer. My greatest confidant. My forever sounding board and biggest cheer-leader. There are not enough words to describe how grateful and lucky I am to not only know you, but to call you my best friend. Thank you for being here for me through all the highs and lows, for always seeing the best in me, for defending me in every situation, and for truly loving and understanding me and my stories in a way no one else could. I love you, friend.

To Becca and Lexy—thank you so much for making me laugh, for supporting me, keeping me on track, and always being in my corner. I'm so grateful for you both.

To the thriller writing community—which, despite what our search histories might suggest, is full of some of the warmest, kindest, most inviting people on the planet.

It is an honor to work alongside of you and call so many of you my friends. Thank you for the laughs, the support, and for continuously elevating our community to new heights.

Last but certainly not least, to you, dear reader—thank you for purchasing this book and supporting my art. All my life, all I've ever wanted to do is tell stories and have people want to read them. By taking a chance on this book, you've helped make that dream a reality. When I write my novels, I'm always thinking of you. I wonder which parts of the story will make you laugh, which parts will make you angry or sad, how you'll feel about the twists, whether you'll figure them out before I mean for you to, and if the ending will leave you satisfied. As always, I truly hope you enjoyed Mari's story. While it certainly wasn't the happiest, I hope you found glimmers of hope and light, moments of humanity to connect to, and maybe even pieces of yourself within the characters. As always, whether this was your first Kiersten Modglin novel or your 41st, my greatest wish is that it was everything you hoped for and nothing like you expected.

ABOUT THE AUTHOR

KIERSTEN MODGLIN is a Top 10 bestselling author of psychological thrillers. Her books have sold over a million copies and been translated into multiple languages. Kiersten is a member of International Thriller Writers, Novelists, Inc., and the Alliance of Independent Authors. She is a KDP Select All-Star and a recipient of *ThrillerFix's* Best Psychological Thriller Award, *Suspense Magazine's* Best Book of 2021 Award, a 2022 Silver Falchion for Best Suspense, and a 2022 Silver Falchion for Best Overall Book of 2021. Kiersten grew up in rural western Kentucky and later relocated to Nashville, Tennessee, where she now lives with her family. Kiersten's readers across the world lovingly refer to her as "KMod." A binge-watching expert, psychology fanatic, and *indoor* enthusiast, Kiersten enjoys rainy days spent with her favorite people and evenings with her nose in a book.

Sign up for Kiersten's newsletter here:
kierstenmodglinauthor.com/nlsignup

Sign up for text alerts from Kiersten here:
kierstenmodglinauthor.com/textalerts

kierstenmodglinauthor.com
www.facebook.com/kierstenmodglinauthor
www.facebook.com/groups/kmodsquad
www.twitter.com/kmodglinauthor
www.instagram.com/kierstenmodglinauthor
www.tiktok.com/@kierstenmodglinauthor
www.goodreads.com/kierstenmodglinauthor
www.bookbub.com/authors/kiersten-modglin

ALSO BY KIERSTEN MODGLIN

<u>STANDALONE NOVELS</u>

Becoming Mrs. Abbott

The List

The Missing Piece

Playing Jenna

The Beginning After

The Better Choice

The Good Neighbors

The Lucky Ones

I Said Yes

The Mother-in-Law

The Dream Job

The Nanny's Secret

The Liar's Wife

My Husband's Secret

The Perfect Getaway

The Roommate

The Missing

Just Married

Our Little Secret

Widow Falls

Missing Daughter

The Reunion

Tell Me the Truth

The Dinner Guests

If You're Reading This...

A Quiet Retreat

The Family Secret

Don't Go Down There

Wait for Dark

You Can Trust Me

Hemlock

Do Not Open

ARRANGEMENT TRILOGY

The Arrangement (Book 1)

The Amendment (Book 2)

The Atonement (Book 3)

THE MESSES SERIES

The Cleaner (Book 1)

The Healer (Book 2)

The Liar (Book 3)

The Prisoner (Book 4)

NOVELLAS

The Long Route: A Lover's Landing Novella

The Stranger in the Woods: A Crimson Falls Novella

Made in the USA
Monee, IL
04 November 2023